Joshua Garrett had changed in the last eight years, Livi thought.

He'd broadened out, no longer the skinny boy he'd been in his teens and early twenties. He was still as beautiful as ever, though he no longer had the messy curls she'd fallen in love with; they'd been tamed into a neat businesslike cut, teamed with a short, neat beard. And he was wearing a formal business suit—expensively cut—instead of the scruffy jeans and worn-into-holes T-shirt with an obscure music reference he'd been wearing the last time she'd seen him. There were tiny lines fanning from the corners of his eyes, as if he spent a lot of time laughing or smiling; he'd lost the brooding intensity she remembered.

Which was probably a good thing.

She'd thought of him as a fallen angel when she was sixteen and sitting in the front row of the Albert Hall, watching him perform. All that beauty, all that talent, the way he'd made her see a skylark soaring up, up, up into the sky as he wielded his bow.

Now, he was just a man.

No. Joshua Garrett could never be *just* a man.

Dear Reader,

I'm a bit of a sucker for second-chance stories, and I was just about to take my husband to Brussels to celebrate a significant birthday when my editor said she'd like a reunion story.

How could I resist? With Belgian chocolate being among the best in the world, I thought a chocolatier/brasserie background would be lovely. (That's my excuse for why we had to visit so many romantic little cafés while we were away.)

Livi and Josh have a lot to work through, with a life-changing backstory in Josh's case. Layers upon layers...just like a perfect chocolate.

I hope you enjoy their story and agree they deserve their sweet ending!

With love,

Kate Hardy

SWEET ON THE CEO AGAIN

KATE HARDY

ROMANCE

Recycling programs for this product may not exist in your area.

ISBN-13: 978-1-335-47075-1

Sweet on the CEO Again

For questions and comments about the quality of this book, please contact us at CustomerService@Harlequin.com.

Harlequin Enterprises ULC
22 Adelaide St. West, 41st Floor
Toronto, Ontario M5H 4E3, Canada
www.Harlequin.com

HarperCollins Publishers
Macken House, 39/40 Mayor Street Upper
Dublin 1, D01 C9W8, Ireland
www.HarperCollins.com

Printed in U.S.A.

Kate Hardy has always loved books and could read before she went to school. She discovered Harlequin books when she was twelve and decided that this was what she wanted to do. When she isn't writing, Kate enjoys reading, cinema, ballroom dancing and the gym. You can contact her via her website, katehardy.com.

Books by Kate Hardy

Harlequin Romance

If the Fairy Tale Fits...

His Strictly Off-Limits Ballerina

The Life-Changing List

A Fake Bride's Guide to Forever

Wedding Deal with Her Rival
Forbidden Kiss with the Prince

Harlequin Medical Romance

Honolulu Medics

The Surgeon's Tropical Temptation

Yorkshire Village Vets

Sparks Fly with the Single Dad

An English Vet in Paris
Pediatrician's Unexpected Second Chance

Visit the Author Profile page
at Harlequin.com for more titles.

To Gerard—
for sharing Brussels (and the chocolate!) with me :) xxx

CHAPTER ONE

'I'VE LEFT THIS pitch until last because I wanted to give the other two a chance to impress us, first,' Michel Lambert said, leaning against the desk in his office at the family's Covent Garden brasserie. Tuesday was usually Livi's day off, but her parents had asked her to swap her shift so she could help with the big project they were working on—bringing the brasserie up to date and expanding the business. Michel had even rearranged the furniture so the office looked more boardroom style, with four chairs around the desk.

'Why would the other agencies need to try harder to impress us, Dad?' Livi asked, not understanding.

'Because we know the CEO of this one,' Sophie said. 'He's your brother's old schoolfriend.'

Even before her mum could say the name, ice slid down Livi's spine.

No.

It couldn't be *him*.

Could it?

She'd spent the last eight years avoiding Joshua Garrett, so she had no idea what he did for a job nowadays. Mutual avoidance, really; the two occasions where they might've been forced together were six years ago at her elder brother Etienne's wedding to Lucy, when Josh had been supposed to be the best man, and two years ago at the christening of Eti and Lucy's daughter Louisa, when she and Josh were both supposed to be godparents. Thankfully, both times, Josh had cancelled very late on, saying that he needed to go into residential therapy for a few days. Livi had been dreading having to face him at the wedding and pretend that everything was perfectly all right between them. It would've been worse still, having the traditional best man and chief bridesmaid dance with him to something smoochy; everyone would still have had their eyes full of metaphorical confetti and started speculating that maybe a romance could blossom between Eti's little sister and his best friend.

When it most definitely couldn't.

Livi had learned that in the harshest possible way, when she was twenty. And she'd kept what happened that night a secret ever since, even from her mum.

'Josh Garrett,' Michel confirmed, making her heart plummet.

When she'd first seen her father's notes, Livi hadn't even considered that 'JGA' might stand for 'Joshua Garrett and Associates.' And right now she was caught between a rock and a hard place. Nobody apart from herself and Josh knew what had really happened between them, that night. If she threw a hissy fit and refused to attend the pitch so she didn't have to face him, her parents would want an explanation—an explanation she wasn't prepared to give. The excuse that it was her day off wouldn't wash, because it was their family business and she'd always been flexible with her time. But if she went to this meeting, how could she possibly behave as if everything was perfectly normal between herself and Josh?

Plus her dad had pretty much hinted just now that he was biased in Josh's favour and was more likely to appoint him than either of the other two agencies.

Livi really didn't want to have to work with the man who'd trampled her heart into tiny pieces.

Though if her father was right and Josh had

indeed become a hotshot marketing guru, and his pitch turned out to be the best of three, she couldn't let her heart get in the way of business either. Insisting on hiring someone whom she knew would be second-best at the job simply wouldn't be fair to the brasserie and their staff.

She'd just have to be professional and keep Josh at a distance.

Somehow.

Josh's palms were actually sweating as he walked through Covent Garden towards Lambert's Brasserie, and there were butterflies in his stomach.

Which was utterly ridiculous. Why on earth was he so nervous? He was good at his job, and he'd worked hard on this pitch. Plus it was for his best friend's family—people he thought of practically as his own family. He wanted to do his best by them, and he thought he'd done that with the marketing plan he'd suggested.

Except he knew that Livi would be there. Not just in the building, which would've been tough enough, but at the pitch itself.

His best friend Etienne's little sister. The woman who had always been off limits. He'd known Olivia Lambert since she was a little girl, and he'd always followed Eti's lead and treated Livi as if she were his own little sister.

Until that night, eight years ago.

Josh had been spiralling deeper and deeper into a black hole after the accident that had ripped his music away from him. The accident that he'd wished at the time had taken his life, instead of leaving him with a left hand that would never be the same again. The surgeon had been brutally honest about it. The average person would've been relieved to have a left hand that still functioned reasonably well, but Josh was a virtuoso violinist, whose left hand needed far more dexterity than the average person's. Even after extensive physiotherapy, his hand simply wouldn't be able to cope with the demands of his job. He wouldn't be able to play the pieces he'd become famous for, the pieces that made his blood sing: not Vaughan Williams' *The Lark Ascending*, nor Paganini's *Caprice Number Twenty-four*, nor the *chaconne* in Bach's *Partita Number Two*.

He'd sat there, trying to absorb the news as the surgeon spoke. That he'd never again transport audiences to another plane at a concert. That he'd never again feel as one with his violin. That the life he'd planned and worked so hard for was over.

A second opinion—and a third—had confirmed it.

He'd never play again.

Not to the standard he was used to, the standard he'd spent his entire life striving for. When you'd sailed through all your exams early, won accolades for your playing, were offered the loan of a Stradivarius, and above all knew that you brought the joy of playing into your audience's heart… Anything less than that couldn't ever be enough.

Josh had given the Stradivarius back—the precious ancient violin he'd been trusted to play by its owner, now cherished by another violinist—and it had felt like ripping out his heart.

The only way he'd been able to cope with such a massive change to his life was to shut everyone out.

Livi had been the one to knock at the door of the flat he hadn't left in weeks. Livi, with those big brown eyes and thick dark hair worn in a messy bob that would make any man want to run his fingers through it. No make-up, no fancy clothes: just jeans and a plain T-shirt, and a Tupperware box containing six different types of cake. She'd smiled at him. 'I'm glad you're in, Josh. I need a favour.'

Josh had stared at her, not understanding. What could she possibly need from him? He had nothing to give. Without his music, he was an empty husk.

Taking his silence as a request to know what she wanted, she'd continued, 'I need you to taste-test this cake for me.' She'd lifted up the box. 'Mum, Dad and Eti want me to enter that TV baking competition. But they're my parents and my brother. They're biased, so I can't trust their judgement and I don't want to make a fool of myself. Am I really good enough to make the grade? I know you'll be honest with me, Josh. And—well, the problem is, I've been dragging my feet about it.' She'd given him a shy little smile. 'The application has to be in tomorrow. Do I go for it or not? I need you to taste this and tell me the truth, right now.'

Part of him had wanted to snarl at her and tell her in very harsh words of one syllable to go away and leave him alone with his despair. Particularly as it was the flimsiest excuse he'd ever heard in his entire life. It was blindingly obvious that his family and friends were so desperate to get him to open up that they'd asked sweet little Livi to try, as a last resort.

Well, tough.

He didn't want to talk.

To anyone.

He just wanted oblivion from the searing loss of his music. Something he'd been lurching towards, hour by aching hour.

But another part of him hadn't been able to resist her request. Something about Olivia Lambert's smile made the world feel brighter—a brightness Josh hadn't been able to see ever since the surgeon had given him the news that had shattered his world and the other doctors had confirmed it. Plus there was always a chance that she might be telling the truth. That she really did need his help. That instead of being Josh the burden, Josh who needed coddling, he could actually do something useful. Something unconnected with music.

He'd caved.

Let her in.

His stomach clenched. Such a wrong move. He should've sent her away. For pity's sake, he'd *known* she'd had a crush on him when she was a teenager. Those puppy-dog eyes, the blush whenever he'd called in to see Eti and she'd been there, the shyness in her smile. He'd always been careful to treat her as Eti's baby sister, even though once or twice he'd glanced in her direction as she laughed and felt a weird zing somewhere in the region of his heart—something he knew he shouldn't act on, so he'd kept his distance.

He should've stuck to his normal resolve, that night, and kept his distance. She should've been *safe* with him.

But he'd been broken, at his lowest ebb. Needy as hell. She'd reached out to him, and he'd reached right back, wanting the comfort she'd offered him. Could she ease the pain in his soul?

He'd taken everything she'd offered, with her full consent.

Afterwards, the enormity of what he'd just done had slammed into him. He'd panicked. And he'd acted atrociously, said cruel things that he knew would make her walk away from him.

They hadn't seen each other since.

He'd apologised to her, a few weeks later, after he'd started therapy. He'd written her a very honest and heartfelt letter, and it had taken him a long time to get the words right; he'd shredded plenty of drafts until he'd finally found the right ones. He'd thanked her for being the catalyst that had finally made him go to therapy and get his head sorted out. And he'd apologised for taking what he shouldn't have taken.

Technically, she'd offered. And she was over the age of consent. They'd both been adults in the eyes of English law.

But he still knew he should've refused. Kindly. He was four years older than her, supposedly more worldly-wise. He should've acted responsibly. Let her down gently. Not taken her to bed. *Definitely not taken her virginity.*

He blew out a breath. She'd never replied to his letter, and he was pretty sure she'd never forgiven him for what he'd said to her that night. In her shoes, he wasn't sure he would've forgiven him, either.

Since then, they'd avoided each other by tacit mutual agreement, somehow without either of their families noticing. Being busy at work was a useful excuse, he'd found—first of all studying for his new career, then going for promotion within the firm, and then finally setting up his own business.

The only sticky bits had been Eti's wedding, six years ago, when things were still so raw, and at Louisa's christening. Of course Josh had said yes when Eti asked him to be the best man. But later that evening Eti had casually mentioned that Livi was going to be the chief bridesmaid. And Josh knew what that meant. A slow dance, in front of everyone. It wouldn't be fair to put her through an ordeal like that. And Josh wasn't selfish enough to make Livi be the one to find an excuse for missing her brother's wedding. It was obvious that he needed to be the one to back out; and it had taken him a while to work out how, without hurting anyone else.

In the end, spending a week in residential rehab—despite not actually having the mental wobble he'd claimed he was having—was the perfect excuse. He'd done the same when Eti had asked him to be godfather. The main thing was that Eti hadn't been hurt; though it had hurt *Josh*. He'd really wanted to be there and share the joy at his best friend's wedding to Lucy and then their daughter's christening instead of being stuck in rehab. Even though Eti had sent him photographs from both celebrations and a slice of wedding cake, it hadn't been the same as actually being there. Being part of the whole thing and making memories together.

Now he had a business meeting with Michel and Sophie Lambert…and with Livi.

Maybe when Michel had asked him to pitch, Josh should've made an excuse. He should've said he was flattered to be asked but he couldn't help the Lamberts because he specialised in other areas. He should've recommended someone else.

But the Lamberts had always been good to him. The way Josh saw it, helping them with their next business move was his chance to pay them back. He wished that Livi wasn't going to be involved with the marketing project, but he needed to be realistic about it. She was their *pâtissière*. If they were going to take some of the options he'd suggested, she'd be in charge of them. So all he could do was be professional, try not to meet her eyes, and do the best he could for the Lamberts.

He came to a halt outside the red-brick building with its Flemish gable, white shuttered windows and discreet gold lettering that proclaimed *Brasserie Lambert*. There were two smart zinc tubs flanking the doorway, each containing a bay tree clipped into a ball; when he went through the door, the interior was all polished cherrywood and chairs upholstered in mulberry-coloured velvet. There were shelves behind the bar showcasing bottles of different Belgian beers along with their specially shaped glasses, and a chalkboard on the wall listed the day's specials. Although it was nearly three o'clock, and the place should've been practically empty, the brasserie still had a few customers who were lingering over coffee and petits fours.

He walked over to where one of the waitresses was cleaning a table. 'Excuse me, please. My name's Josh Garrett, and I have an appointment with Mr and Mrs Lambert in a couple of minutes. Could you let them know I've arrived, please?'

'Sure,' she said, returning his smile and disappearing behind the bar area.

And Josh told himself that his heartbeat was only rocketing because it was adrenalin making him sharp for the pitch. It had nothing to do with the prospect of seeing Livi again for the first time since that night.

He ignored the disappointment flickering through his veins when Michel Lambert was the one to come out to greet him. Of course Livi wouldn't have been the one to collect him.

'Josh! Good to see you,' the older man said with a broad smile. 'Come through to the office.' He shepherded Josh into the small room that held a table and four chairs set out in the style of a boardroom.

Sophie Lambert—an older version of her daughter, with those same dark eyes but with her grey hair tamed into a sleek bob—stood up and greeted him warmly. 'Josh. Thank you for coming. Livi's just sorting out a tray of coffee.'

Livi. His heart skipped a beat.

It was just pre-performance nerves, he told himself, which was a good thing because it meant he wasn't taking anything for granted. Just as, back in the days when he'd been on stage, he'd never taken his audience for granted. He'd always given everything.

He could do this.

He took his laptop from his briefcase, switched it on, brought up the presentation and turned the laptop so the screen was facing the Lamberts.

When Livi walked through the door a couple of minutes later, carrying a tray with four mugs, a jug of coffee, and a plate of delicious-looking chocolates, he managed to ignore the way his heart skipped a beat and gave her his most professional smile.

She inclined her head. 'Good afternoon, Joshua.'

Ouch.

She'd always called him by the short version of his name that everyone used. Using his full first name was clearly her way of signalling to him that she'd make an effort to sound friendly for her father's sake, but she intended to keep things strictly businesslike and formal between them.

Fair enough. It was more than he deserved. 'Good to see you, Olivia,' he said, using her own full name as a way of telegraphing back that he'd match her professionalism. The tiny nod of her head told him that they had a truce. For now.

She'd changed in the last eight years, he thought. She'd lost her shyness, meeting his gaze with no hint of a blush; she had an aura of calmness and self-containment. And this new, confident Olivia was incredibly attractive. Her dark hair was caught back in a ponytail—clearly for hygiene purposes at work, because she was also wearing a white chef's jacket and black-and-white patterned trousers.

Her eyes were the same, though. So dark he could drown in them.

But he didn't have the right to think of her in those terms. The way he'd treated her had ruined his chances of having any kind of relationship with her. Besides, she was twenty-eight now. The chances were, she was in a long-term relationship with someone. Someone who would treat her a lot better than he had, he thought with a stab of guilt.

He accepted a mug of coffee, added his own milk, and waited for the Lamberts to sit down before he began.

'Thank you for giving JGA the chance to pitch for the business,' he said. 'I've read the brief thoroughly, and the way I see it you have three possibilities for expansion. I'll cover those in my presentation, and then perhaps we can discuss my suggestions and you can ask me any questions the presentation raises for you.'

Joshua Garrett had changed in the last eight years, Livi thought. He'd broadened out, no longer the skinny boy he'd been in his teens and early twenties. He was still as beautiful as ever, though he no longer had the messy dark curls she'd fallen in love with; they'd been tamed into a neat businesslike cut, teamed with a short neat beard. And he was wearing a formal business suit—expensively cut—instead of the black velvet tailcoat, silk bow tie and wing-tip shirt he'd worn while playing at a concert, or the scruffy jeans and worn-into-holes T-shirt with an obscure music reference that he'd been wearing the last time she'd seen him. There were tiny lines fanning from the corners of his cornflower-blue eyes, as if he spent a lot of time laughing or smiling; he'd lost the brooding intensity she remembered.

Which was probably a good thing.

She'd thought of Josh as a fallen angel, when she was sixteen and sitting in the front row of the Royal Albert Hall, watching him perform. All that beauty, all that talent, the way he'd made her see a skylark soaring up, up, up into the sky as he wielded his bow.

Now, he was just a man.

No. Of course he wasn't. Joshua Garrett could never be *just* a man. Not to her. But he was still easy on the eye. And he had a warmth and professionalism she hadn't quite expected. As he went through the presentation, she could see exactly why Josh's agency had won awards. He'd read the brief thoroughly, and it was clear that he'd asked her parents some supplementary questions before he'd even started working on it, checked out their competition, and seen the gaps in the market that they could fill. He'd looked at the possibility of franchising the brasserie, as well as simply adding new branches in a rolling programme of expansion.

'You have distinct sets of clients at the brasserie: the ones who come for business lunches, the ones who come for pre-theatre dinners, and then those who want a romantic dinner or a family meal later in the evening,' he said. 'You're known for good quality, authentic Belgian food and beer. You could easily turn Lambert's into a chain or a franchise, keeping this brasserie as the flagship, and the other branches would follow the same pattern. Maybe they could offer different specials of the day so your chefs feel they have some creative say in what's produced,' he added.

He'd thought of the staff? Of the fact that a chef needed to feel untrammelled? That was impressive, too, Livi thought. The other agencies hadn't even touched on that.

'But you also have gaps,' he continued. 'As part of running the restaurant, it makes sense to have quieter times where you can focus on preparation. But I think you could also make those gaps work for you. You could fill them here, or you could do a sideways expansion.'

'What kind of gaps?' Sophie asked.

'Mid-morning coffee and pastries, brunch, and afternoon tea,' he said. 'A sideways expansion would be a café rather than a brasserie, but using the Lambert name and design to make it clear that it's part of the same business and has the same attention to quality. Like the brasserie, the café would do things the Belgian way. Coffee with waffles or pastries in the morning. Tartines—' open-faced sandwiches '—as part of brunch, with options of savoury waffles and maybe a spectacular cake. And afternoon tea with a Belgian twist.'

As Lambert's *pâtissière*, Livi had originally suggested expanding their range of desserts, and she'd wanted to launch a range of handmade chocolates—she'd been testing them out with coffee after meals, and they'd gone down well with customers. She hadn't thought of moving sideways and opening a café, with a completely different menu, where she could offer cakes and patisserie creations… Even though she'd intended to stay professional and cool, she couldn't help sitting a little straighter and asking, 'What do you mean by a Belgian twist?'

'Traditional English afternoon tea is sandwiches, scones, cake and something in a "verre",' he said. 'Swap the sandwiches for mini *croque monsieurs*, and the cakes for mini Belgian specialities—waffles, *speculoos* biscuits, the cake of the day and a fruit tart or a frangipane. Make the "verre" a Belgian chocolate mousse, or swap it for a couple of handmade pralines.'

'And the scones?'

His smile made her heart skip a beat. 'Ah, you need to keep them. We're in England, and an afternoon tea wouldn't be a proper afternoon tea without warm scones. But maybe offer a choice of different jams or spreads—ones that might not usually be offered in England.'

'A Belgian twist. Cherry jam, blueberry, and maybe apricot,' she said thoughtfully.

He held her gaze. 'Your dad said you were thinking about producing a range of chocolates. You could have a takeaway counter in the café, for the pastries and for chocolates. Test what your customers like, and then maybe offer mail order if you want to expand into other items. Chocolates, waffles, and *speculoos* biscuits with the Lambert's logo stamped on them.'

'It's something to think about,' she said coolly, though inside her mind was racing. He'd pretty much nailed the things she'd been thinking about—things that the other two candidates had ignored, focusing solely on turning the brasserie into a chain.

This was something they could test at the brasserie without having the start-up costs of a café. Josh was right about the gaps in their offerings: morning coffee and pastries, and afternoon tea. And brunch would help them blend seamlessly from breakfast into lunch. They'd need to juggle staff rotas a bit, but it was doable. If it was a success, then they could open a café in its own right, which could perhaps double as a bar in the evening and offer a much more casual limited menu of mussels, steak and *frites*.

Her parents had a few more questions, and Josh answered honestly; she appreciated the fact he actually said he didn't know the answer to one of them, but he'd find out and get back to them later that day. She remembered that the other two agencies had bluffed, which had annoyed her.

'Any more questions?' Michel asked his wife and daughter at the end.

Sophie and Livi shook their heads.

'Then if you wouldn't mind waiting a few minutes, Josh, I need a quick confab with my business partners,' Michel said with a smile.

'Shall I see you in the bar, when you're ready?' Josh suggested.

'That'd be great. Do you need Livi to show you out?'

'It's fine. I know my way,' he said, to Livi's relief—or was there a tiny bit of disappointment blurring the edges, too?

She shook herself.

Not now. Wrong time, wrong place, and *definitely* the wrong man.

The second the door had shut behind Josh, Michel said, 'That was the best presentation out of the three, by far.'

'I agree,' Sophie said.

Livi knew that if anyone other than Joshua Garrett had given that presentation, she would've picked the agency. Disagreeing and picking someone who wasn't as good—solely because they weren't Josh—would be the wrong thing to do for the business. It looked as if she would just have to do her best to work with Josh, and somehow try to minimise her interactions with him. 'OK,' she said.

'I know he still has to come back with some figures for us, but I think we should hire him,' Michel said.

'Livi, I think he had a great point about the café. And that would give you room to try new things,' Sophie said. 'If there are any masterclasses you fancy, now's the time to book them.'

That would be a perfect get-out, Livi thought. She could be away on a course any time she had to deal with Josh. 'I'd love that, Mum. Thanks. And I was thinking, maybe I should do a fact-finding mission when I'm in Brussels for the chocolate course. Obviously I can do an internet search, but seeing things for myself means I'll have better ideas about what's on offer, what's popular with customers, and what kind of tweaks I can do here in London.'

Sophie smiled. 'Great idea, darling.'

'I think,' Michel said, 'we should put you in charge of the expansion.'

What? Now that she hadn't expected. In charge in the kitchen for the café expansion, perhaps. But her mum had always done front of house and her dad had always been the main chef, just as her grandmother had been front of house and her grandfather had been the chef before them, and her great-grandparents before *them*. 'But the brasserie's yours and Mum's,' Livi protested. If there were going to be any changes, surely her dad wanted to oversee them?

His next words told her exactly how he felt. 'We're both getting to the point where we think it's time to hand over to the next generation,' Michel said. 'Eti decided to take a different career direction, and he's happy in his work, so I'm not expecting him to drop everything to run Lambert's. Besides, asking him to run the business wouldn't be fair on you; you've worked hard, in every area of the business, and you know inside out how things work. The staff all know that and they respect you. Putting you in charge will be the right choice for everyone.'

On the one hand, this was huge. Everything she'd worked towards. Her parents were trusting her with the family business and letting her choose its direction. She'd be in control, knowing that she'd worked her way up and earned the role. And the bit that really made her feel good was that her dad sounded so proud of her. She knew she'd let her parents down, picking too many Mr Wrong-for-hers and not managing to settle down with anyone the way her brother had with Lucy, but where the business was concerned she could make her family proud of her.

On the other hand, it meant there was no way she could get out of working with Josh.

'Livi?' Sophie's forehead creased with concern.

Livi forced herself to smile. 'Sorry. I wasn't expecting it, that's all.'

'It's your turn to shine, *ma petite*,' Michel said. 'We're not stepping away and abandoning you completely. You'll have our full support in anything you need. But your mum and I have talked about it for a while, now. We think it's time to step back. We talked to Eti about it, and he agrees with us.'

Even though her brother didn't work in the family business, his support was appreciated. 'Thank you for trusting me,' Livi said.

'You've earned it,' Sophie said.

'Let's go and tell Josh the good news,' Michel said.

CHAPTER TWO

'YOU REALLY DON'T need me around for this bit,' Livi said, trying not to panic. 'Anyway, I have things to do in the kitchen.'

'I'll step in for you and keep things ticking over,' Sophie said. 'Your dad's right. This is going to be your show, so you should be the one to tell Josh and brief him for the next stage.'

'I need to pop out and see one of our suppliers,' Michel said, 'so you can use the office.'

From anyone else, Livi would've suspected a set-up. But her parents wouldn't do that to her. They genuinely still thought Josh, as their son's best friend, got on OK with their daughter, and besides this meeting was all about their business.

Livi was relieved they didn't know what had happened between herself and Josh. She still felt a squirm of shame every time she thought of that night. Right now her face felt hot and her skin felt too tight. But what choice did she have? She didn't want to burst her parents' bubble, so she'd have to play along.

'Why don't all three of us tell him?' she suggested. 'And then I can book in a meeting with him to discuss the way forward.' By which time she would've managed to get a smooth, sophisticated mask in place and could deal with the situation.

'All right,' Michel agreed.

But clearly her parents had really meant it about her being in charge of the project, because when they met Josh in the bar area her dad smiled. 'Livi has news for you.'

'You've won the pitch,' she said, hoping she looked and sounded a lot cooler than she felt. 'And I'm the one who'll be taking things forward.'

Livi was going to be in charge? Josh blinked. That was something he hadn't expected. He'd known she'd be part of the project—of course she would, given that she was the brasserie's pastry chef. But her dad had said nothing about stepping down from the helm of the business or taking a lower profile. If Livi was in charge of the project at the brasserie's end, it meant that Josh would be working much more closely with her than he'd anticipated.

How did she feel about it, given that she'd sent him that coded message earlier with the use of his formal name rather than the short version everyone used? Right now, her expression was inscrutable and he didn't have a clue what was going on in her head.

'That's good,' he said carefully. 'Thank you. I look forward to working with you, Olivia.'

'If you wanted to make a start,' Sophie said, 'Michel's about to go out and I can take over from Livi, so the office is free.'

He noticed Livi's eyes widening slightly. She seemed a bit reluctant to be in a meeting with him this afternoon. But maybe this was what they needed. A quiet, private space where they could talk properly and decide how they were going to handle this. And this time he'd say that apology to her face instead of hiding behind a letter.

'We can at least agree the next couple of steps,' he said.

Livi gave a sharp nod of agreement. 'I'll try to be as quick as I can, Mum.'

'Take your time, darling,' Sophie said with a smile. 'See you later, Josh.'

'Thank you again for choosing JGA, Monsieur and Madame Lambert,' Josh said.

'There wasn't any nepotism involved, if that's what you're thinking. Yours was the best pitch.' Michel chuckled. 'And we're still Michel and Sophie, to you. Even if we weren't, I prefer business footings to be on first-name terms, just as Livi does.'

'Michel and Sophie,' Josh echoed with a smile.

He followed Livi in silence back to the office where he'd pitched to all three of the Lamberts, and closed the door behind him. 'I think we need to talk,' he said.

'Yes.' Her face was tight with anxiety, and that made him feel even more guilty.

'We need to clear things up between us,' he said, 'and decide where we want to go from here.' Suddenly, it felt as if there wasn't enough air in the room. But he wasn't a coward. He'd face up to what he'd done. 'Obviously your family knew you were coming to see me, that night—but you didn't tell them what happened between us, did you?' If she had, he was pretty sure that either Eti or Michel would've confronted him at the time.

'I just said you didn't let me in.' She shrugged.

'They assumed that meant not letting me into your flat.'

Whereas she'd actually meant that he hadn't opened up to her. Hadn't talked to her, the way he should've done. Hadn't told her the deep, dark secret he hadn't even told his therapist.

'I didn't deserve that protection,' he said, 'but I appreciate it. And I'm truly sorry for hurting you, that night, Livi.' He swallowed hard. 'I have no excuse, though I do have an explanation. When you came to my flat, I really wasn't in a good place.' Which was the understatement of the century. He'd been shattered, raging at the universe and feeling as if he was right at the bottom of a dark, hopeless well. He hadn't been able to see a future in front of him, not without his music. 'But I still shouldn't have taken out my misery on you. You're Eti's little sister. You should've been perfectly safe with me.'

Colour flared into her face, but she said nothing.

'I apologise for everything,' he said. Everything he'd done. Everything he'd said. 'I did write you a letter of apology, a few weeks later—after I'd had a few sessions of therapy and finally started to get my head round the accident.'

'I got the letter,' she said. 'But I never read it.'

Had she recognised his handwriting and thrown it straight into the bin? Well, he could hardly blame her. If it had been the other way round, he wouldn't have wanted to listen to anything she had to say, either. 'I'm ashamed of the way I treated you,' he said. 'I wasn't coping with the aftermath of the accident. I couldn't handle knowing that everything I'd always wanted to do with my life was over. Permanently.' Her expression was still completely inscrutable. Clearly he'd blown it, so he might as well go the whole way. 'It doesn't excuse what I did to you—there is no excuse for that—but, as I said, it's an explanation. I'd pushed everyone away and managed to keep them at a distance. I'm assuming that's why my parents and Eti were desperate enough to ask you to try using cake to get through to me.'

'Yes,' she confirmed.

She'd agreed to help because she was a decent person, and that made him feel even worse. 'When I saw you on the doorstep, it was the first time I'd felt anything—other than being in a black hole—since the crash. I didn't want to let that feeling go. That's why I kissed you.' She'd offered him cake and he'd kissed her. He swallowed hard. 'I shouldn't have done it. I shouldn't have taken you to bed.'

Taken her to bed, and taken her virginity.

Though it had been with her consent. Livi knew she needed to be fair about that. 'You gave me the chance to say no,' she said. 'I could've said no at any point, and you would've listened.'

'Thank you for that,' he said. 'But I'm still firmly in the wrong. You were vulnerable. You were only twenty, and you'd never even left home,' he said softly. 'I was older than you. I'd lived away from home during my degree course, and I'd travelled the world for my job. I knew you were sheltered. I should've been more responsible. Afterwards, when I realised you were a virgin and I'd taken something precious from you, something I didn't deserve, I panicked. I didn't want anything more than—well, just that night. I was terrified when it occurred to me that you might want more than that. Something I couldn't give you. And I said some unforgiveable things to you.'

Was that what he'd written in his letter?

Livi remembered every searing bit of shame and embarrassment as he'd told her that he didn't want her. How scornful he'd sounded.

How stupid she'd felt, thinking that she might be able to be the one to reach him through the wall of his misery and save him from himself—thinking that he might be glad of her help, and then they might become friends in their own right, and then one day he might notice her as more than just his best friend's little sister and realise they were perfect for each other…

Instead, he'd made it very clear that she wasn't what he wanted. At all. She was little more than a schoolgirl, in his eyes.

And maybe he'd had a point. When it boiled down to it, she'd had the equivalent of a teenage crush on a man who wasn't who she thought he was. A selfish, spoiled, entitled manchild. And how stupid had she been not to see that when it was so blindingly obvious?

The humiliation still felt as fresh and stinging now as it had back then. Even though she was nearly a decade older.

'Did you…' Her voice sounded cracked, and she cleared her throat, not wanting him to know how much it still hurt. 'Did you know I had a crush on you?'

'Since we're clearing the air and being honest—yes, I did,' he said, and then Livi *really* wanted the earth to open up and swallow her. 'But I'd also known you for years and years. If I'd been in my right mind at the time, I would've treated you as I always did: as Eti's little sister. I would've treated you how I would've wanted anyone to treat my own little sister, if I actually had one.' He gave her a rueful smile. 'I would have made it very clear that nothing other than friendship was ever going to happen between you and me. But I wouldn't have been cruel about it.'

That night, he *had* been cruel. He'd sneered at her, asked her why on earth she thought he'd want someone like her.

'I should've treated you with the respect you deserved,' he said quietly. 'Instead, I used you to anaesthetise the feelings I couldn't handle.'

He'd had sex with her. Taken her virginity. Then he'd gone cold on her.

'I felt guilty. I knew I was in the wrong. I said things I didn't actually mean, to stop myself from feeling anything at all. And I'm sorry for hurting you. It was incredibly unkind, and I'll always regret the way I behaved,' he said. 'That's why I didn't go to Eti's wedding or Louisa's christening. It wouldn't have been fair to you, pretending everything was all right between us, when it wasn't.'

She'd always wondered why he'd really

called off being the best man, only a couple of weeks before the wedding. 'Did you lie about needing to go to therapy?'

He wrinkled his nose. 'Not completely. I did go to residential therapy, that week, even though strictly speaking I was managing OK at the time. But I knew it was an iron-clad excuse that Eti would accept without digging any deeper, and that would leave you in the clear.'

He'd avoided the wedding and the christening because of her. He'd been sensitive. And that was a shock, because in her head it brought Josh back to being the man she'd always thought he was, rather than the one she'd encountered that night in his flat and considered him to be ever since.

'So that leaves us here,' he said. 'Working together on the future of Lambert's Brasserie.' He looked her straight in the eye. 'I didn't know you were going to be in charge of the project when your dad asked me to pitch. I thought you might be involved, but I also thought we'd manage to find a way round it so we could avoid each other. If you'd rather not work with me, I understand completely. I'll find an excuse to step back from the project and make it clear to your parents that it's my fault, not yours. Or I could delegate almost everything to my team. They're good people and they'll do their best for Lambert's. I'll oversee things my end, but you won't have to deal with me personally.'

'They're the options?' she asked. 'You resign from the project, or you delegate?'

'There is a third option—and I'm well aware that it's asking a lot,' he said.

She folded her arms and waited for him to tell her.

'We could try to put the past behind us,' he said quietly. 'We could work together to make Lambert's have the future you want it to have.'

Put the past behind us.

It had been eight years ago. She'd been young and impossibly naïve. He'd been broken, failing to come to terms with losing the future he'd planned for himself.

They'd been different people. It had been another life. They'd both moved on.

And now he was giving her the choice. No pressure. He'd made it clear that he would accept her decision rather than try to charm his way round her.

She thought about it.

She thought about it for so long that he said softly, 'Livi? I'm not the person I was, that night. Talking therapy has helped me a lot.

And I owe you a huge debt for that, because that night was what made me realise I'd hit rock bottom and things wouldn't get better unless I accepted help. I'm only sorry that you were the one who took the brunt of my pain and my anger.' He blew out a breath. 'I was massively unfair to you. Unkind. And I'm truly sorry about it. What I did, what I said—it was all unforgiveable. I wish I could go back in time and change things.'

And give her back her virginity, too? Of course he couldn't, and they both knew it.

'But maybe we can find a way to make the business side of things work, for your parents' sake,' he finished.

She looked him straight in the eyes. That blueness she'd once mooned over was full of sincerity. She could see that he really did regret hurting her, back then. That night, he'd taken everything she'd offered, then thrown it back in her face because he'd been in too much pain to appreciate what she'd given him.

But now he'd owned up to his mistakes. And he'd been honest about the fact that, at the time, he'd been in a bad place, unable to come to terms with losing the career he loved—that he'd put everything into. It hadn't been just a job, had it? Where the arts were concerned, it was a vocation: what you did was who you were. Thanks to the accident, Josh had lost his identity as well. She'd known all that before she'd even knocked on his door. Her beloved older brother had told her how worried everyone was about him, how Josh had gone in on himself and nobody could reach him. And she'd seen herself as the equivalent of a knight in shining armour, armed with cake to chase his demons away…

What would she do, if she couldn't cook anymore? If, say, she lost her sense of taste and smell, and couldn't be certain that even an old recipe that she could virtually make in her sleep had worked properly? How would she react if everything she loved doing was ripped away from her?

She'd always been aware of the age gap between them, but maybe four years wasn't that huge. At the time of his accident, Josh definitely hadn't had the maturity to deal with what had happened to him; but would anyone have been able to cope with that at the age of twenty-four? He'd been heading for the top, tipped as being the best violinist since Paganini. He should've had decades of playing and success in front of him.

It had all been ripped away in a few seconds—because someone in another car had decided to drive after a few drinks, ending up on the wrong side of the road and smashing into the car in which Josh had been a passenger. Irony of horrible ironies, the driver who'd caused the accident had walked away without a scratch. Meanwhile Josh had lost everything. His incredible talent. His music.

'Do you miss it still?' she asked.

'Yes,' he said. 'It's not as raw as it was, but that hole will always be there. A missing piece of me.' He gave her a lopsided smile. 'Sometimes I have incredibly vivid dreams—in colour, with sound—and I think I can play again. Then I wake up, and it takes me a while to adjust. Luckily my therapist gave me some good tools for coping.'

'You don't play at all, now? Not even a little bit?'

'When I'll never be able to play the way I used to?' He shook his head. 'That'd hurt more than not playing at all.' He paused for a moment, clearly thinking about it. 'Say you couldn't make your favourite dishes ever again or learn a new technique. All you could do was boil an egg, and even then you'd need a bit of help to scoop the egg out of the pan. Would you have the heart to do that? Stick to the confines of just one very simple recipe, never again being able to create one of your incredible pastries?'

How did he know her pastries were incredible?

Then again, he'd clearly done his research into the brasserie. Maybe he'd even eaten here without her knowing and sampled one or more of her desserts. But the compliment pleased her, the more because he clearly hadn't been trying to compliment her. He was trying to make her understand how he was dealing with his limitations.

Could she handle the situation he'd just outlined?

She thought about it. 'Not cooking at all would be easier to handle than only having the most limited repertoire,' she admitted. Now she could understand why he avoided what had once been his entire life. 'So you retrained.'

'I found something I could do,' he said. 'I'm lucky. I got a second chance. And even though I admit I'd trade it all in a heartbeat for just one night playing on stage the way I used to…' He shrugged. 'It's not going to happen, so there's no point in breaking my heart over it. And there are bits of my job that keep me going. My team.' He smiled. 'Maybe it's daft, but it makes me feel like a proud mother hen when my babies get a bit more confidence and try new things. And I always encourage them when it comes to job enrichment. It makes everything better for everyone.'

'Mother hen.' She couldn't help chuckling at the idea. Josh was the least hen-like person she'd ever met.

'Seriously. Roosters aren't involved in the care and upbringing of the chicks,' he said. 'Before you ask, I know that because I have a client who runs a farm park. She taught me a lot about her animals. And it's got nothing to do with gender. I'd rather be the mother hen who encourages my babies and notices when they achieve something, than the rooster who's full of noise but doesn't actually do anything for them.'

Which was exactly how she ran her bit of the kitchen. She liked hearing her team's ideas and giving them the chance to practise a new skill. Maybe she and Josh had more in common than she'd thought.

He hadn't mentioned his personal life, she noticed. There was no wedding ring on his left hand—not that *that* meant anything. Not all men wore rings; and you didn't have to be married to be committed to someone. 'I'm glad you've found a way through,' she said.

'I was lucky to find a good therapist who understood what made me tick, and helped me learn to deal with things. The whole process made me realise how close I'd come to…' He broke off, and a muscle flickered in his jaw. 'Well. It is what it is.' He took a deep breath. 'I owe you an apology, Livi,' he said softly. 'And I'm sorry it's taken me so long to face you. I should've had the guts to come and apologise in person, years ago.'

She hadn't read his letter because she hadn't wanted to see in black and white any expression of regret for something that had meant something to her. 'I'm not sure I would've agreed to see you, years ago,' she said. She'd almost backed out of the meeting today.

'I don't blame you,' he said. 'And I hope you've found someone who appreciates you the way you deserve to be appreciated.'

How had he managed to arrow in on the one thing she knew she'd failed at—the one thing where she'd let her family down? Her brother Eti was happily married, with a little girl. Her parents were happily married—they'd been together since they were eighteen. And there she was, with a string of broken relationships behind her and an inability to commit. Most of the time, she'd been the one to call a halt; but sometimes, just when she'd thought she might finally be able to open up and let someone in, her partners had given up waiting for her and dumped her.

She narrowed her eyes at him. 'You don't need to be in a relationship to have a successful life.'

'I know. I didn't mean to imply otherwise.' He raked a hand through his hair, displacing his curls slightly, and that tiny bit of scruffiness made him look much less polished—and dangerously sexy.

Livi had to remind herself that she couldn't afford to let herself think like that about him, ever again.

'I guess what I mean is I hope how I treated you didn't put you off. Relationships, I mean.'

Was he asking if she was single? Hitting on her? Now? Was he being just a little bit patronising, thinking he'd put her off love? Or was she being oversensitive because she knew she was a failure at relationships, and ascribing motives to him that he didn't actually have? 'That's irrelevant to the project,' she muttered.

He winced. 'Sorry. It wasn't my intention

to pry.' He lifted his chin. 'And you don't owe me absolution.'

'I'm glad we've got that straight,' she said, doing her best to sound cool and collected and not as if he'd just stoked up an old fire.

He winced again. 'I'm not normally this clueless or inarticulate. Livi, can we maybe start again, please? Even though we've known each other for years, I think we stopped knowing each other eight years ago—which is entirely my fault. But we're both different people now. Older. Wiser. Wanting different things from life.' He held one hand out to her. 'This time round, it'll be strictly business. I want to do my best for Lambert's. You're my client and you're trusting me with your company's future. I want to do my best for you, as a professional.'

She believed him.

And this Joshua Garrett—the thoughtful marketing guru who'd come to terms with his past and who went to bat for his entire team rather than just ordering them around—was a man she thought she might be able to work with.

'I want the best for Lambert's, too. I think we're on the same page,' she said, and took his hand. She shook it firmly. 'It's a truce.'

'Good,' he said. 'I'll look at what your nearest competitors are offering for afternoon tea—and I mean cafés rather than the upmarket hotels. Then perhaps we can sit down and work out what Lambert's can offer to make it different.'

'Actually, I've already suggested that to my parents.' The next words bubbled out before she could stop them. 'Maybe we should do the research together.'

He blinked, and she felt warmth flood into her cheeks. She didn't want him taking this the wrong way, as if she was suggesting a date. Because she absolutely wasn't. Dating Joshua Garrett might have been her absolute dream as a teenager, but it wasn't the case anymore. 'What I mean is, you can learn the basics of what a company offers from their website, but you can only judge their quality and the ambience if you actually visit them and try the product.'

He nodded. 'You're right. And it makes sense to work together. Your view will be that of a service provider, whereas mine would be that of a customer. Between us, we'll cover all the bases.' He paused. 'How about we both make a list of the five strongest competitors, then compare the list tomorrow, put them in order, and work through the list one a day for the next week?'

'Like a late business lunch,' she said. If she said the b-word often enough it might squash any more of these ridiculous thoughts that were threatening to surface. 'Works for me. What about your diary?'

'If necessary, I can move things. I'll send you my list later this afternoon.' He handed her a business card. 'Here's my work phone and email. If you can message me your contact details, that'd be useful. Let me know which competitors you want to start with and which times are good for you, and I'll book something.' He paused. 'Thank you for giving me a second chance.'

Second chance?

Her pulse sped up for a moment.

No, of course he didn't mean that kind of second chance. He meant not letting their past get in the way of their business relationship.

Except then he shook her hand again, and her palm tingled where he'd touched it. Oh, help. She definitely needed to ignore this lingering awareness of him. Nothing, absolutely *nothing*, was going to happen between them, this time around. She wouldn't take that risk again. 'You're welcome,' she said, trying to keep her tone entirely professional. 'Let me see you out.'

'No need. I know my way,' he said. 'I won't take up any of your time unnecessarily.'

She felt a twinge of disappointment. Which was utterly ridiculous, because there was no reason for her to feel disappointed at not being in his company. 'I'll message you later,' she said, as coolly as she could.

And it really didn't help when he smiled at her. A proper, genuine smile. One that made her heart feel as if it had done an award-winning gymnastics routine.

She was going to have to be really, really careful.

CHAPTER THREE

OLIVIA LAMBERT HAD grown up, and Josh really liked the woman she'd become: quiet, thoughtful and honest. She still had that warmth that had attracted him so much on the long dark night of his soul. Until that night, he'd never even really seen her as a woman; she'd simply been Eti's little sister. He'd been focused on his career, not his love life. But now he looked back and remembered times when he *had* noticed her—when she'd been laughing at a joke, or that sweetness in her smile had suddenly pierced his consciousness and he'd felt that weird little throb in the region of his heart.

Livi was obviously still Eti's little sister, but the four-year age gap didn't matter anymore. And she drew him. Every bit of his common sense told him to put this out of his head, because she was off limits, but he couldn't ignore that zing of attraction.

He was still none the wiser about whether

she was involved with someone. Not that it was any of his business. He'd more or less asked her outright, and she'd set him straight. *That's irrelevant to the project.*

Of course it was.

But he still wanted to know. Had she found someone to cherish her, treat her the way she deserved and undo the damage he knew he'd done to her all those years ago? Was she happy?

He could hardly ask her parents. Or Eti. They'd want to know why, and he didn't want to tell them the truth.

Maybe the internet would give him a clue, he thought. But her social media profile turned out to be so low-key it was untrue. Livi had clearly had a hand in some of the posts for Lambert's Brasserie, but she wasn't on any social media as herself. That, or she'd locked down her profile details securely so that nosey strangers—such as he was, right now—couldn't find her at all.

She was right about it being irrelevant. Even if she *was* single, nothing was going to happen between himself and Livi. She was his client. End of. And he'd just have to stop thinking about the way his skin had tingled today when she'd shaken his hand.

'She's off limits,' he told himself out loud, earning himself a funny look from the woman sitting next to him on the Tube. He gave her an apologetic smile and resisted the urge to explain. Given that he couldn't work out his feelings himself, he could hardly lay them out for a complete stranger.

No, what he needed was to bury himself in some work. As soon as he was back in the office, he'd brainstorm some ideas with his team. Focus on his job. And he'd definitely stop thinking about Olivia Lambert.

Livi needed to get her game face on before she went back to the kitchen to take over from her mother, because she knew Sophie would have questions. She also knew that her mother was well aware of her old teenage crush on Josh; and that her parents both worried she was too focused on her job and never dated anyone for long. Half the time when her brother invited her for dinner, it wasn't because Eti wanted her to bring dessert. He and Lucy, her sister-in-law, had tried pairing her off with a few of their suitable single male friends until Livi had gently explained that she wasn't desperately looking for Mr Right—or Ms Right, for that matter—and was quite happy with her life as it was.

Just please don't let her parents get the bright idea that Josh would be perfect for her and try to throw them together, she begged silently. She could hardly tell them that she already knew he was Mr Wrong, because then she'd have to explain why. They could all do without that particular grenade being lobbed into the mix.

Josh had actually told her he hoped he hadn't put her off relationships. She'd brushed the comment aside, but now she thought about it, part of her was irritated. Then again, she didn't think he was driven by arrogance or a desire to patronise her. She rather thought it might be guilt that had made him say it, because he knew he'd treated her badly.

And he also had a point. Nobody she'd dated had ever matched up to the Josh of her dreams; ironically, that included Josh himself, and she hadn't even *dated* him. She'd simply had sex with him, which wasn't the same thing at all.

Although Livi had been attracted to a few of her boyfriends enough to spend the night with them, she'd quickly realised she didn't want to spend the rest of her life with them and had broken it off. There hadn't been any depth to her feelings, and it wasn't fair to continue a relationship when she knew it didn't have any kind of future. Others, she hadn't even let close. They'd all been Mr Wrong-for-her. And the ones that maybe could have made it…well, they'd dumped her.

Now she considered all those failed romances. Had she perhaps blocked off her feelings on purpose, so nobody would get the chance to disappoint her the way Josh had? Had she dumped them—with a couple of exceptions—before they'd had a chance to dump her? Was he right, and she'd let her experience with him put her off falling in love with anyone?

She shook herself. This wasn't about her love life, or the lack of it. This was about expanding the family business. Nothing more. And she wasn't going to let Josh unsettle her—even though he might be right when he'd said that they were both very different people from the last time they'd met. She was going to treat him like she would any other business acquaintance: fairly and politely, but staying detached.

Thus determined, she did a mental trawl through the local cafés that would be their nearest competitors and made a quick list. This was the perfect thing to distract her parents, if they asked her about Josh. They could maybe add to her list. She put them in a rough order, added her own contact details, then checked Josh's business card for his email address and sent the list to him along with a note saying that she could be free for an hour after two p.m.

Then—because the business card listed JGA's website—on impulse she looked up his company.

At thirty-two, Josh seemed to be the second oldest in his team. His office manager looked like everyone's favourite aunt; but his social media and SEO manager, the campaigns manager, the research guru and the digital marketing manager all looked almost fresh out of university. He had a designer, a photographer and a wordsmith; and in the candid shots on the website it was clear that they all loved their jobs and the team was closely knit.

His social media outside work was non-existent. Then again, she wasn't surprised. The last thing he needed was for people to work out who he used to be and ask when he was going to start playing again. Unless any of his clients were classical music fans, they probably wouldn't connect him with Joshua Garrett the violinist. She smiled wryly. Not that she was one to talk. She didn't bother with it, either, outside the Lambert's social media accounts. She enjoyed scrolling through certain foodie accounts just for the videos, but she'd rather spend her free time reading—or experimenting in the kitchen in her flat.

She wasn't going to ask her brother about him, either. Lucy would overhear, put two and two together and make five—and then invite both of them round to dinner. Awkward, awkward, awkward. And it wasn't any of her business whether Josh was involved with someone or not.

She'd just logged off the computer and was about to slide her phone back in her pocket when it pinged with a message.

Josh.

The message was a copy of the booking receipt for one of her nearest competitors in Covent Garden; it would be a two-minute walk for her, though he'd need to come in from either the JGA office at King's Cross, or his flat in Bloomsbury—if he still lived there. Not that that was relevant. Or any of her business.

Have booked afternoon tea for two at 2.15 tomorrow. Let me know if not convenient. J.

He'd given her a ready-made excuse to chicken out.

Though she had no intention of using it. It made sense to do this particular research together; it would give her extra feedback from a customer's point of view. And it had been her idea, after all. This was business. What could go wrong?

Is fine. Thank you for booking, she replied. And then, because she really *was* curious about his life now, she added, If your partner wants to join us, that's fine. L.

If he was attached, then that would be yet another good reason to keep her distance and make sure her old feelings for him stayed in the past, where they belonged.

His reply, later that afternoon, didn't give her the answer she'd fished for. I don't have a business partner at JGA. But thank you. J.

Livi managed to keep all thoughts of Josh out of her head until after the lunchtime rush the following day. And then she went up to her flat above the restaurant, changed into a summery dress, and found herself applying make-up.

Oh, for pity's sake. This was a business meeting; she was the client, so it didn't actually matter what she wore. She absolutely didn't need to try to impress Josh Garrett.

Cross with herself, she wiped off the make-up and kept her hair in the ponytail, the way she wore it for work, rather than taking it down. Josh was already there, sitting at a table waiting for her as she crossed the square and walked into the café at fourteen minutes past two.

He stood up politely and waited for her to take her seat before sitting again.

Those manners would be the death of her. Truly old-fashioned: and so, so sweet.

'Good afternoon, Livi. I took the liberty of doing a spreadsheet,' he said, 'so we can analyse the components more easily.'

Very businesslike. Just what she should've done. 'That's a good idea.' Livi gave him a professional smile. 'Actually, I had a mental checklist.'

'Want to hit me with it, so I can compare it with mine and amend the spreadsheet?' he asked.

She lifted an eyebrow. 'Don't you trust me to amend the spreadsheet?'

'Fair point,' he said, and passed his phone to her.

She scanned what he'd listed: contents of

the tea, split by type of food; ratings for quality and quantity; what drinks were on offer; whether refills were offered; if there were options or it was a set menu; price. 'That's fair, from a consumer's point of view,' she said. 'You've listed what you get for afternoon tea and how much choice you have.'

'Anything you'd add?'

'From my point of view, we need to look at presentation,' she said. 'Do they use a cake stand, plates or a slate? Is the tableware matching, vintage or plain? Is everything brought out at once or is it staggered? Are the scones warm or cold? If there's a choice of cake, do customers choose at the counter, from a menu, or is a selection brought over on a trolley?'

'That would obviously affect how things are plated and how much work it makes for the staff,' he said thoughtfully. 'Which I didn't consider. Do you want to add them in?'

'It's your spreadsheet and your tech,' she said, 'so it makes sense for you to do it.'

There was a flicker of amusement in his gorgeous blue eyes as she handed the phone back to him without actually entering anything.

'I learned a long time ago to pick my battles

wisely,' she said, steepling her fingers. 'By the way, because this is my idea, it's my bill.'

'It's client research,' he corrected. 'Making it my bill.'

'And then it'll be part of your expenses,' she said, 'meaning the brasserie will be paying VAT twice. No.'

He grinned. 'No flies on you.'

'I'm not just a…' she began, and stopped halfway through the hackneyed phrase. *Not just a pretty face*. She wasn't even that, according to the man sitting opposite her. She was a stupid, spotty-faced schoolgirl playing dress-up. It made her regret wearing a dress now; and she was relieved that she'd wiped off the make-up before she left her flat.

Maybe Josh had become a lot more perceptive, because he seemed to guess the thoughts she hadn't said. 'From what I've seen of you, Olivia Lambert,' he said quietly, 'you're capable of doing anything you put your mind to, whether it's making those amazing desserts or running a business empire. Though personally I think you'd be wise to hire a business manager to handle the stuff you don't enjoy doing as much. It's a better use of your time to do what you love and delegate what you don't.'

Josh had once loved what he did for a living. His music had been his life. And when the accident had taken that away from him, it had broken him.

Not that they were going to discuss that.

She mumbled something anodyne and glanced through the menu. 'So it looks as if we get sandwiches, scones, a savoury, cakes and a verre. Choice of five different types of tea or filter coffee. Set menu. OK.'

When the waitress came over, she ordered a pot of Earl Grey; Josh ordered green tea with lemon.

'Pretty china,' she said approvingly when the teapots arrived. 'And it's looseleaf tea.'

'I need to add that in,' Josh said. 'In case some of them don't offer looseleaf.'

'Some places use silver teapots rather than china,' she said. 'Though I think that would be more the high-end afternoon tea they'd serve at a posh hotel, which isn't the market I'm aiming for.'

'Agreed,' he said, and added in the comments she'd made earlier.

The sandwiches were excellent, and talking about the food meant they didn't touch on anything personal. But then they ran out of business to discuss.

She needed to make small talk. Something

not too personal. 'Did you come from the office, or were you working from home this morning?' she asked.

'The office,' he said. 'I don't tend to work from home that often. I focus better with people around me.' He looked at her. 'Do you still live with your parents?'

'I moved out a couple of years ago. There's a flat right above the brasserie,' she said. 'Which means I don't have a commute.' She paused. 'Are you still in Bloomsbury?'

He shook his head. 'I sold the flat and moved back home when I first went to rehab. I stayed with my parents until I'd finished retraining.'

Completely understandable, she thought. There would be too many memories in his old place.

'I live in Bayswater now,' he finished.

'A flashy penthouse in a Georgian building?' she guessed.

'A three-bedroomed mews house, not far from Hyde Park,' he corrected. 'Cobbled street, lots of greenery outside—one of my neighbours is very keen on the Mews In Bloom stuff and nags us all into taking part. I'm not a gardener, so I pay him to do it for me.' He smiled. 'The house has been renovated so it has a modern kitchen-cum-living room, but it still has most of its historic character.'

'There's a lot to be said for historic character,' she said. 'My flat's only a one-bed, but it's full of light and I'm right in the middle of Covent Garden.'

'Just round the corner from St Martin-in-the-Fields.' His voice was soft, but it held a world of pain.

She remembered when he'd played a candlelight concert in the church. She'd gone with Eti to watch Josh as a soloist, and she'd been spellbound. The way Josh had moved as he played had made it look as if the violin was actually part of him.

How much he must still miss it, even though he'd made a new and successful life for himself.

'It's also close to all the big theatres and the National Gallery.' She decided not to mention the Royal Opera House. She was pretty sure Josh had played on that stage, too, and avoided it now. 'And I'm not that far from St James's Park, which is a nice walk in summer.' She looked at him. 'What made you decide to move to Bayswater?' If he was near Hyde Park, that meant he lived within walking distance from the Royal Albert Hall—which he'd once told her was his favourite place in London. Another stage where he'd conquered the world. Surely it was too close for comfort?

'I liked the house,' he said. 'And it's an easy Tube journey to work. A ten-minute walk to Paddington station, and no need to change lines.'

'You didn't fancy a posh warehouse in King's Cross overlooking the canal, then, so you could walk to work?' she asked, striving for lightness.

'No. I did think seriously about Notting Hill,' he said. 'I nearly put an offer on one of the ice-cream-coloured houses. But then the mews house came up. I went for a viewing and it just felt…' He spread his hands. 'As soon as I walked in, I knew I was home.'

'That's how I feel about my flat, too,' she said.

A one-bedroomed flat—one that she'd said was quite small, although it was smack in the middle of Covent Garden and that made it a desirable piece of real estate. If Livi was involved with someone and was thinking about moving in with them, she'd probably need more space. She hadn't mentioned needing more space, so it sounded as if she was single. Josh really hoped that was by her personal choice, and not because he'd put her off relationships. He'd asked her, earlier, and she'd batted it aside. Maybe he needed to be a bit more explicit.

'You mentioned my non-existent business partner joining us for research,' he said. 'Did you want yours to join us?'

'Mum and Dad? No. They're happy to leave this to me,' she said. 'Though they did make a couple of suggestions for places we should check out. I've made a note. I'll send it on to you.'

'Thank you.' He still didn't have the answer he wanted. Obviously he was going to have to be a little bit more explicit. 'And your non-business partner is OK with you more or less having lunch with me exclusively for the next week?'

'Is yours?' she countered.

He should've guessed she'd answer a question with another question, batting it back to him. OK. If she wanted him to answer first, it was the least he could do. He owed her. 'I don't have a non-business partner.' Before the accident, he'd been too focused on his career to think about his love life. Afterwards, following rehab, he'd dated sporadically, but nobody had drawn him enough to make him want to make the relationship last. He'd been careful to end things kindly—he'd learned that much from what had happened with Livi—so he was still on good terms with his exes, but he hadn't let anyone close enough to think about any kind of future with them. 'I've been busy changing my career, studying and getting the media company up and running.' Using work as his excuse to keep his distance from relationships.

'Me, too. Well, I haven't changed careers, but I've been busy with the restaurant,' she said. 'Everything from shadowing Mum on the admin side through to taking full responsibility for the dessert menu, and teaching my skills to my team.'

So she *was* single. Because of how he'd treated her? Or because she hadn't found the person who lit up her world? Part of him felt guilty, because she deserved more than that. Another part of him was pleased, because if they were both single he could act on that pull he felt towards her. And yet another part of him was worried that this was a really bad idea, because he'd been a failure at relationships these last few years and he didn't want to get involved with her only to let her down again.

As if the questions showed on his face, she said, 'I think we can agree that we're coming from a similar place.'

'Yes,' he said.

Her phone beeped with what sounded like an alarm. 'That's me due back to the brasserie,' she said. 'I could stay out a bit longer, as this technically counts as work, but I don't want to put needless pressure on my team.'

'Of course. I'll fill in my bit of the spreadsheet and send you the link to a shared document. Or you can send me your notes and I'll collate it—whatever works best for you,' he said. 'I'll book somewhere for tomorrow and send you the details. Same time?'

'Same time is good. Thanks. I'll sort the bill on my way out,' she said.

'OK. See you tomorrow,' he replied.

He wasn't sure whether he was more relieved or disappointed when she didn't shake his hand. But he lingered thoughtfully over the remainder of his pot of tea. This was the new start he'd asked her for. The question was, where did they go from here?

CHAPTER FOUR

'I MEANT TO ask you when your days off are, so I don't take up your free time,' Josh said to Livi on Friday, after they'd finished their late lunch and discussed the menu thoroughly.

'Monday and Tuesdays,' she said.

He blinked. 'You work every weekend?'

'Saturdays and Sundays are busy days in restaurant terms,' she said. 'I'll fill in on a Monday or Tuesday if we're short—and obviously there was your pitch on Tuesday, this week—but usually that's my equivalent of a weekend.'

'I need to book our next afternoon tea for Wednesday, then,' he said.

'Actually, I don't mind doing them on Monday and Tuesday,' she said. 'I don't have anything in particular planned next week.'

Her day off. Which meant she would be free to spend a decent part of the day with him, not just a one-hour slot with the occasional messaging flurry in between. An idea bloomed in his head; even though part of him knew he shouldn't be mixing business with pleasure, it was too irresistible to turn down. Because he really wanted to get to know Livi better. 'How about,' he asked carefully, 'we go off-piste?'

Her eyes narrowed. 'How do you mean?'

'There's a new heritage venue just opened not far from me,' he said. 'A Regency house, set up how it would've been back in the day. There's a revolving exhibition of clothes on loan from the V&A. If I remember rightly, you were a bit of a Jane Austen fiend in your teens.'

She looked surprised. 'You remember that?'

He chuckled. 'I remember Eti complaining about your parents' living room being taken over by a posse of teenage girls arguing over which was the best adaptation of *Pride and Prejudice* and watching all of them back to back, the summer you were seventeen.'

'I remember that,' she said, smiling. 'And Mum kept us all going with tea and cake.' She widened her eyes at him. 'Actually, the bank where Austen's brother Henry was a partner is just round the corner from Lambert's. Jane herself stayed at the flat above the bank when she was working on the proofs of *Mansfield Park*.'

'Henrietta Street,' he said. 'She wrote to her sister Cassandra in 1813 that the flat was "all dirt & confusion, but in a very promising way".'

'You know that?' She blinked. 'You're an Austen fan, then?'

'Yes and no,' he said. '*Mansfield Park* was one of my A level texts. I absolutely hated it. But I get Austen's importance, and my mum likes costume dramas. I've kept her company watching some of them.' And he'd had to try very hard to tune out the music. Not that he was going to tell Livi that. He didn't want her sympathy—or, worse, her pity. 'Anyway, I thought it might be interesting to have a look round. Apparently the garden's fabulous. There are guided tours of the house twice a day, and the exhibition and gardens are both open a bit longer. They have a tearoom. It'd be good to see what they do with afternoon tea.'

'You're thinking Regency afternoon tea? Nope. Strictly speaking, afternoon tea wasn't invented until the 1840s,' she pointed out.

'By Anna Maria Russell, the seventh Duchess of Bedford,' he said.

She gave a wry chuckle. 'I should've realised that you'd do your homework.'

'Of course. That's why I also know that in Regency times women were more likely to drink tea than coffee.'

'Hmm,' she said. 'You're edging into show-off territory, now.'

'Thoroughness,' he corrected. And then he thought better of it. What had she said about picking her battles wisely? 'Anyway, I thought maybe we could enjoy an anachronistic afternoon tea after a look round the house and garden.'

It wasn't an official date. It was a continuation of their research, he told himself. And he hoped she'd see it that way, too.

'All right. If nothing else, it'll be a palate cleanser,' she said. 'Something different.'

'Good. And this one's on me—because it's slightly off-piste, and because it's my suggestion.'

For a moment, he thought she was going to argue. But then she smiled. 'Thank you. That'll be lovely. What time?'

'The house tours are at eleven and two,' he said.

'Let's go for the eleven o'clock,' she suggested.

'Paddington's the nearest Tube. Meet you by the Paddington Bear statue on Platform One at ten forty-five?' he asked.

'Perfect,' she said.

Weird how her smile made him feel warm all over. And weirder still how he kept thinking about her all over the weekend.

Apart from the briefing meeting, they'd spent all of three hours together. They'd eaten and discussed three afternoon teas together. Everything had been strictly business.

But he'd also learned a lot about the woman Livi had become during those three meetings. She was kind. Tactful—she'd asked him about his music, but she hadn't pushed. She thought about things before she made a decision, analysing them properly.

Then there was his physical reaction to her. Eti's little sister, all grown up. No longer the awkward, shy twenty-year-old she'd once been; now she was comfortable in her own skin. That confidence alone would make her beautiful; but when you added the warmth of her personality, she *glowed*.

If he had any sense, he'd find an excuse to stay out of her way.

But she drew him. Not like a moth to a flame, because Livi wasn't about pain. More like a butterfly to the sun, he thought, because her warmth made everyone around her feel that the world was a better place.

Maybe their new start could change things between them. Maybe they could get to know each other as they were now. Put the past behind them, where it belonged. And then maybe they could see where things took them…

On Monday morning, Josh walked to Paddington station and stood near the bronze statue of the bear just before quarter to eleven, making sure he wasn't in the way of families wanting to take photographs of their children next to the statue. He saw Livi walking towards him across the platform; she was dressed for sightseeing in comfortable shoes, black trousers, a pretty summer top and a sunhat.

'That was a good suggestion for a meeting point. It was easy to find,' she said, and her smile made his heart squeeze.

He desperately wanted to tell her how lovely she looked, but held it in. 'Thanks for coming,' he said instead, hoping he sounded professional and nothing like the hot mess of his feelings. Part of him knew that he shouldn't be blurring the lines between them—that he should be sticking to a business relationship with her and not thinking about anything else. But he found Livi hard to resist. Her warmth made him feel things he hadn't felt for years, and it made him want to explore that further.

'Well, it was a choice between doing this or doing chores. A nosey round a historic house and garden and the promise of good cake won. Just,' she said, giving him a sidelong look.

He couldn't help smiling at the tease. 'I should hope so.'

The heritage house wasn't far; there was a group of ten on the tour, and he and Livi were the youngest by a generation. But he enjoyed walking round the house, listening to what the guide had to say.

'Oh, I love this room,' Livi whispered as they went into the library. 'I can really imagine living here. It'd be the perfect place to curl up and read for an hour.'

So she liked reading, still? He wondered what she read, apart from Austen.

Most of the walls in the library were covered by glass-fronted mahogany cabinets full of books; there were drawing room chairs with gilded arms and comfortable red velvet upholstery, and little tables dotted about. Josh could imagine a room like this being updated with modern reading lamps. 'It's easy to imagine living here,' he agreed.

The dining room was very grand, with duck-egg-blue walls, a marble fireplace, an ornate plaster and gilt ceiling and chandeliers. There was a large mahogany table with sixteen chairs in the centre of the room, and there were dishes piled with incredibly realistic-looking replica foods.

'Service *à la Française*,' Livi said. 'The dishes were served all at the same time—more or less like a buffet, and you'd be helped to the dishes nearest you. The first remove was joints and sides, then they'd clear the table completely and bring in the second remove of fish, poultry, pies and puddings. The most important guests would have the fanciest dishes close to them, and the least important would get the poorer dishes to choose from.'

'Didn't the servants do the—well, serving?' Josh asked.

'If they carried the dishes round like they do today, that was known as service *à la Russe*,' she said. 'But *à la Française* was the usual way. The thing I couldn't get my head round, though, was that if you doubled the number of guests, instead of just doubling the quantity you'd make double the number of different dishes.'

'That sounds like a lot of work,' he said. 'And the potential for a lot of waste.'

'Not necessarily wasteful. They'd reheat the leftovers, the next day,' she said.

'How do you know all this?' he asked. 'Did you study the history of food as part of your training?'

'No. Holly, my best friend, is a history teacher, and she's fascinated by food in history,' Livi said. 'I've been to a few exhibitions with her—including seeing the carbonised bread they found in Pompeii—and we've done a couple of special Jane Austen days where we dressed up in Regency outfits and had dinner and a ball.' She smiled. 'I'm definitely going to send her photos of this place. She'll love it.'

Livi was clearly enjoying their outing, and he was really glad he'd suggested it. Until they went into the next room; he felt himself freeze as he realised that this was the music room. The room itself was gorgeous, with sky blue walls and comfortable sofas; the plasterwork on the fireplace and ceiling was a little plainer than that in the other rooms, as were the chandeliers. There was a piano to one side of the fireplace, and a harp on the other: the perfect space for performing. And on an occasional table there was a violin propped up in its open case. Something that made his fingertips itch and his heart ache.

Josh did his best to keep his expression neutral, but Livi clearly noticed because she took his hand and squeezed it briefly. Pity? But when he glanced at her, it was empathy he saw in her eyes. He gave her a rueful smile, hoping she'd know he appreciated the support.

He was relieved when they were taken through to the withdrawing room with its crimson silk damask wallpaper, the ballroom, the bedchambers with an extraordinary array of clothes, and finally below stairs to the kitchen and scullery. At least then he didn't have to think about music and the massive hole at the centre of his life.

At the end of the tour, they were able to wander through the gardens at their leisure. It was a beautiful space with a rose arbour and rich herbaceous borders; some of the paths were in bright sunlight, and there were several benches set in shady corners. The orangery at the far side of the garden had been converted into a tearoom, and Josh was delighted to see that among the bistro tables and chairs there were actually a couple of orange trees in large terracotta pots. They ordered afternoon tea for two and found a quiet table.

'That's definitely one of the most liveable period houses I've ever seen,' she said. 'Would you have liked to live during Regency times?'

He thought about it. 'No. If you were poor, you had very few choices and a tough time trying to keep your family alive and fed. If you were at the other end of the social scale, then you were stuck spending your time with the *ton*.' He shook his head. 'I think they would've seriously annoyed me. A bunch of entitled people, bored out of their skulls and spreading vicious gossip because they had nothing else to fill their minds—because of course gentlemen couldn't *possibly* do some work.' He grimaced. 'Can you imagine being forced to put up with people you really didn't like for days on end, just because they were of the same social class as you and you were supposed to invite them to your house party and entertain them?'

'For me, it's all the restrictions on what you were allowed to do, the rules and regulations, that would put me off,' Livi said. 'I would've had no independence. I would've been expected either to marry—meaning the minute I got married, my husband would take ownership of all my possessions and I'd be nothing more than his chattel—or to be a companion to someone who expected me to do everything they wanted and be grateful for the opportunity.' She shuddered. 'And, as you say, the endless house parties. Being forced to sew or draw when you had no talent or interest in it, because that's what women were supposed to do. Listening to people singing out of key and having to be polite about it—or, worse, hearing other people rip them to shreds behind their back.'

'Or listening to someone playing the piano or the harp really badly.' He grimaced. 'Maybe I'm being territorial or over-fussy, but I really wouldn't be happy about someone ham-fisted sitting down at my piano and bashing out a tune. I'd want the instrument respected.'

'No, that's fair,' she said. 'The *ton* were an entitled lot. Pushy parents and desperate debutantes, all chasing the money. I know they were a product of their time, but I think I would rather have stayed on the fringes. I would've preferred to be with the bluestockings.'

'So,' he said, 'would I.' Clever women who thought about what they said—like the one who was sitting opposite him right now and who tactfully hadn't brought up the way he'd frozen in the music room. And he needed to acknowledge what she'd done. How her warmth had thawed him again. 'And thank you,' he said quietly, 'for understanding what was going through my head in the music room.'

'No problem,' she said.

He almost—*almost*—reached across the table to take her hand.

But this wasn't the time or the place. Even though he wanted to change things between them—to get to know her properly, become friends and maybe then start dating—he'd promised her that their relationship would be strictly professional. It was the least he owed her. He needed to back off and keep things light between them. He went back to their discussion about the Regency. 'All the fussiness around clothes back then would've driven me mad, too. Employing people specifically to dress you, for pity's sake! I can't get my head round that.'

'To be fair, zips hadn't been invented,' she pointed out. 'Women needed someone else to do up those buttons down the back of their dresses.'

Josh wished she hadn't said that. Because

even though he was trying to damp down those growing feelings towards her, her words had put a picture in his head and now he was thinking about what it would be like to undo a row of buttons down her spine, kissing every centimetre of skin as he revealed it. And he really hoped she didn't have a clue what was going through his mind. She'd run a mile.

Thankfully, the waitress came over with their afternoon tea at that point and they switched the conversation back to work. But he was still incredibly aware of Livi. The curve of her lower lip. The length of her eyelashes. The way her eyes crinkled at the corners when she laughed. He wanted to walk with her to a quiet spot in the garden. Take her hand. Press a kiss into her palm. Move his mouth upwards and feel the pulse in her wrist beating against his lips…

Focus, Josh. That's not our deal, he reminded himself.

But the more time he spent in Livi's company, the more he realised he liked her. *Really* liked her. Provided she felt the same way as he did, could they make it work? The gap between their ages wasn't an issue any longer; she was a woman in her own right and he should see her as that, rather than just his best friend's little sister.

The sticking point, though, was that night.

How much he'd hurt her, when he'd pushed her away. It would be hard for anyone to forgive that.

But they were both different people now. If he asked her—maybe told her the truth about what almost happened, that night—would she give him a second chance?

Even after they'd left the house and gardens and he'd gone back to work, he couldn't stop thinking about her. His office manager, Shelley, even called him out for daydreaming, and he had to think on his feet to come up with something even vaguely resembling a valid excuse.

At the end of the week, they'd finished working through Livi's list of competitors. All Josh had to do was finish collating their thoughts and write a report. Then he realised that it meant he had no real reason to see Livi, which in turn made him realise how much he *did* want to see her again. He'd enjoyed their lunch dates—well, business meetings, he corrected. He hoped that she had, too. They hadn't found themselves at cross purposes; if anything, he'd felt they'd been in tune with each other.

So maybe, he thought, just maybe, he should talk it over with her. Tell her his feelings had changed. Ask her on a proper date.

And she might even say yes.

Josh was still mulling over what he'd suggest as a first proper date when his phone pinged with a message; and his heart skipped a beat when he realised it was from Livi. Was she thinking about him, too? he wondered. Did she feel this same odd mixture of shyness and wariness and need?

He flicked into the message.

Been thinking. Need guinea pigs.

Not quite following her train of thought, he sent an immediate reply: ??

This time, she responded by calling him. 'Is this an OK time to talk?' she checked.

'Yes. What's the guinea pig stuff about?'

'I've worked out my afternoon tea menu, but I need some people to taste-test it—and not my family or Holly, because they're biased—even if they tried not to be, they wouldn't be able to help themselves. I need someone neutral,' she said. 'I was thinking, maybe I could drop in to your office on Monday lunchtime and your team can give me an honest opinion of the food?'

'That's an excellent idea,' he said. Especially as it gave him a very valid excuse to see her again.

'That's settled, then. I need to know how many people are in your team, any allergies or food intolerances, how many are vegan or veggie, and if there's anything they won't eat,' she said. 'Don't worry, you don't have to remember all that. I'll text you. But would you be able to let me know the answers by, say, the end of play today?'

He smiled. 'I imagine you already know that kind of information about your own team.'

'Well, yes,' she said. 'Of course I do.'

'Snap,' he said. 'So I can give you the answers right now. Nobody in my team has any food allergies or intolerances. There are ten of us, including me. Two are vegans and two are veggies; of the rest, one hates fish and one hates egg sandwiches. They all love chocolate, if you wanted to test your pralines on them.'

'Perfect,' she said. 'Next question. Do you have a staff kitchen?'

'You're planning to cook everything at my office?'

'Possibly some of it,' she said. 'The alternative is using a thermal bag to keep things hot. What facilities do you have?'

'A microwave, an oven with a hob and grill, and an air fryer,' he said. 'We also have a good coffee machine and a kettle.'

'Perfect. I can work with that,' she said. 'What time does everyone break for lunch?'

'Usually it's flexible,' he said. 'Tell me what time you want everyone there, and I'll make sure they are.'

'I'll take over your kitchen at twelve,' she said, 'and serve at one.'

'OK,' he said. 'Do you want me to put together a questionnaire so we can analyse their responses?'

'That's probably quicker than asking them and recording their answers, isn't it?' she asked.

'Yes,' he said. 'I'll draft something and have it with you by tomorrow morning.'

'Great. Thanks,' she said. 'I'll look forward to that—and I'll see you on Monday.'

Monday, Josh thought, was going to be an excellent day.

CHAPTER FIVE

ON MONDAY MORNING, Josh texted Livi and asked her to call him five minutes before she arrived, so he could meet her at the door and help her bring in the supplies. He had to force himself to focus on the new brief he was working on, because his thoughts kept straying to Livi and how he felt about seeing her again. Which was ridiculous; he was a sensible thirty-two-year-old man with workaholic tendencies. Yet he felt as giddy as a fifteen-year-old boy waiting to meet his new girlfriend after school. Giddier, because at fifteen Josh had been much more focused on his music than on girls.

Finally she called him. 'See you in five.'

'Be right there,' he said, and he was outside the front door of the office when the black cab pulled up.

'What do you need me to carry?' he asked.

'This crate, please,' she said, pointing to one

of the two crates in the back of the taxi. 'It's the china, cutlery, skillet and baking trays.'

It was surprisingly heavy, but then again he supposed it was for ten people.

She carried the other crate, which Josh surmised was the food.

'So this is your office,' she said, outside the glass door with 'JGA' written in discreet script.

'It's open plan, with a boardroom and a couple of breakout rooms, plus the kitchen and bathrooms,' Josh said. 'Let me introduce you to everyone.'

He set the crate on his own desk, and his team crowded round.

'Lovely to meet you, Miss Lambert. This is going to be such a treat,' Shelley, the office manager, said. 'I've been to your brasserie a few times with Elinor, my partner, and the food's always amazing.'

'Thank you,' Livi said, smiling. 'We've got a really good team at the brasserie. And we're all excited about the new direction.'

'What can we do to help?' Indira, the designer, asked.

'Nothing. I'm making you all work through your lunchbreak, and that's enough,' Livi said cheerfully.

'Stuffing our faces doesn't feel like work,' Indira said. 'It's going to be a pleasure.'

'I thought we'd eat in the boardroom,' Josh said. 'Do you want us to lay the table?'

'No, it's fine. It'll be quicker for me to do it than to talk you through it,' she said. 'Show me where the boardroom and kitchen are, and you don't have to babysit me. Just all be ready for one o'clock, please. And if someone could do me a list of what drinks everyone wants, I'll bring out the tea and coffee at the start.'

Once Josh had helped her carry the crates to the kitchen and shown her to the boardroom, he followed her instructions and left her to get on with things. Keep it professional and don't get under her feet, he reminded himself.

At five to one, he ushered the team into the boardroom. She'd set up the table with a runner in the centre; the plates were on placemats, and the cups and saucers on coasters. In front of each place setting was the questionnaire he'd designed with her.

A couple of minutes later, she came in with a tray containing a teapot, a coffee-pot, a sugar bowl and a jug of milk. She looked every inch the professional in her dark trousers and double-breasted chef's coat, and her hair was pinned up below a dark red skullcap.

'Thank you all for agreeing to be my guinea pigs today,' she said. 'As I'm sure Josh has already told you, this is a test run for the afternoon tea I'm planning to serve at Lambert's, so it has a Belgian twist. At the brasserie, I'm planning to use tiered servers, but for today I'm using large plates and I'd like you all to try as many of the different options as you can, please. You've probably already looked at the questionnaire by your place setting—Josh and I thought this would help us analyse your responses more quickly—and it's up to you whether you do them as you go or fill them in at the end. I'd like to emphasise that I'd like honest responses, please; I won't be upset or offended if there's something you don't like about the meal. I need to know what works and what needs tweaking.'

She was clear and precise; Josh thoroughly approved of the way she was running this.

'Please help yourself to drinks,' she said. 'I'll be back with the first lot of savouries.'

By the time everyone had filled their cups, she was back with the first two plates. 'Josh suggested that instead of finger sandwiches, I should serve warm Belgian sandwiches. So we're starting with mini *croque monsieurs* and tartines. They're all on sourdough bread, which I made this morning. The standard *croque monsieurs* are cheese and ham, and the vegan ones are smoky aubergine and smoked vegan cheddar. Enjoy, and I'll bring the next plates in.'

It was definitely the best *croque monsieur* Josh had ever eaten, and that included ones in Paris.

When she returned to the boardroom, every scrap of food had been eaten. 'Next up, the tartines. They're basically open-faced sandwiches, on toasted bread. I have a grilled vegetable and hummus version here, and a fig and prosciutto; I'll bring the tomato and vegan Boursin next, plus smoked salmon and pickled cucumber.' She swapped the new plates for the empty ones, then brought the other tartines through.

'Aren't you eating with us?' Pete, the photographer, asked.

'No, I'm fine,' she said with a smile. 'I'm simply here to serve the food and answer any questions.'

But she did at least need a drink. Josh decided to go for the professional approach. 'When I run focus groups, where people will be talking a lot, I always make sure drinks are available—particularly for the group leaders or any presenters,' he said. 'Can I get you a glass of water or a cup of tea?'

'Tea would be lovely, please,' she said.

He poured her a cup of tea the way he'd learned that she liked it. She gave him a warm smile that made his heart do a backflip.

When the savouries were all gone, she brought in warm scones and dishes of butter, cream and jam. 'They're all vegan scones today, and it's vegan butter,' she said, 'simply because that makes everything easy. I plan to offer dairy and non-dairy versions. The coconut cream's in the blue bowl and the clotted cream in the yellow bowl, depending on whether you want dairy or not. The jams are cherry, blueberry and apricot, and the colours make it obvious which one's which.'

'It's all amazing,' Jenna, one of the two vegans, said. 'I'm going to be telling everyone I know about this when you start serving afternoon tea at the brasserie, because they really need to try this. And I run a food blog. I'd love to do a piece on you when you open.'

'That'd be great,' Livi said with a smile. 'And you can perhaps direct me. I do the occasional photo or menu for the brasserie's blog, but I don't do videos.'

'A video of you making the scones would

be awesome,' Jenna said. 'But I'll shut up now and make notes on your questionnaire.' She grinned. 'I don't want to miss out on eating time!'

Next, Livi brought in the sweet section. 'This first lot are all vegan, so they're suitable for everyone here. The *speculoos* are traditional Belgian biscuits made with caramelised sugar and Ceylon cinnamon, so they should taste slightly orangey. The waffles have a drizzle of dark Belgian chocolate. The cream-coloured macarons are vanilla, and the green ones are pistachio. Finally, the brownies are made with dark chocolate.'

And every single morsel that Josh tried was delicious.

She followed up with a tray of bite-sized gateaux. 'Mango mousse and passion fruit curd; raspberry mousse and lemon curd; mini salted caramel eclairs,' she said, gesturing to them in turn. 'I'm afraid the only vegan-friendly cakes here are the strawberry tartlets, but I'm going to work on vegan versions of the others.'

'Good,' Jenna said. 'Because they look stunning.'

Josh thought of the cake Livi had offered him, eight years before. If he'd only eaten it and opened up to her, talked properly instead of pushing her away…

He shook himself. Not now.

Finally, she brought in the verres and a plate of pralines. 'This is Belgian chocolate mousse. The vegan ones are made with coconut cream, and they have a solid chocolate V rather than an L on the top,' she said, gesturing to the stylised letters she'd clearly drawn in chocolate.

'L for Livi?' Peter asked.

'L for Lambert,' she said with a smile.

'You can buy letters made out of chocolate?' Indira asked.

'I made them,' Livi explained. 'With melted dark chocolate on a teaspoon. It takes a bit of practice, but once you get the hang of it it's easy. Oh, and the pralines are vegan-friendly. I made them this morning, too.'

'I have never, ever had such good food,' Jenna said. 'I'm not sure whether I want you to marry me or adopt me!'

'Me, too,' Peter said.

'Wait your turn in the queue, you two,' Indira said. 'I think we all feel the same.'

Livi chuckled, clearly enjoying their banter. 'Well, it's good to know you like the food.'

'Love it, more like,' Jamal, Josh's wordsmith, said. 'Any time you need someone to test things for you, I'm more than happy to be there.'

'When you open the café, are you going to offer takeaway as well as dining in?' Shelley asked. 'Elinor works at King's College, and she'd definitely buy sandwiches and cake from you.'

'I haven't thought quite that far, yet,' Livi said. 'We're starting with a soft launch at the brasserie so we can gauge the demand. If it goes the way I hope, then we'll open a dedicated café as well as a second branch of the brasserie. And maybe we'll sell ballotins of pralines at the café and the brasseries.'

'I'll make a note,' Josh said.

'Definitely sell the chocolates,' Peter said. 'Add them to the menu so people can order them and take them home after their meal. Mail order via the brasserie website is another possibility we came up with when we were brainstorming ideas. These are seriously good.' He paused. 'If the jam's home-made, you could sell that as well.'

'I hadn't thought about jams,' Livi admitted.

'Another note,' Josh said with a grin.

She accepted a mug of coffee and sat chatting to Josh's team until they'd finished eating the cakes and the mousses. They insisted on doing the washing up, and Josh ordered a taxi back to Covent Garden for her.

'That was a definite success,' he said outside the office as they waited for the cab to turn up. 'I'll analyse the questionnaires, this afternoon, and give you a report first thing tomorrow morning.' He looked at her. 'Actually—maybe we can discuss it over dinner, tomorrow night? I'll cook for you, if you like.'

She widened her eyes at him. 'That's brave. Most people would worry about cooking for a professional chef.'

'I didn't say it was going to be a fancy dinner,' he said. 'And I'm definitely not trying to compete with you. It'll only be something simple.'

She smiled—and he loved the way that smile reached her eyes. 'Simple food is often the best food.'

'And there's no way I'm even going to try impressing you with a dessert. I'm not going to pull the wool over your eyes, either—I can tell you now it'll be fruit and ice cream bought from my local deli,' he added.

'I love fruit and ice cream. There's nothing nicer in the summer,' she said.

'Any allergies or major dislikes I need to know about?' he checked.

'No. What time do you want me to arrive?' she asked.

'Would seven work for you?' he asked.

'That's fine. The only thing I need now is your address,' she said.

'I'll send it over tomorrow with the report,' he said. 'Thanks again for making us part of your research, Livi. The team were blown away by the food—and that includes me.'

He was rewarded by another smile, revealing the cutest dimples. How had he never noticed them before? And how was he going to get the picture of said dimples out of his head and concentrate for the rest of the afternoon?

CHAPTER SIX

JOSH KEPT HIS PROMISE, sending Livi the report and his address on Tuesday morning. His team had come up with a lot of thoughtful comments and suggestions, and Livi started to feel confident that the soft launch was going to work well.

But she was having second thoughts about Josh cooking for her in his home. This was blurring the boundaries. They were supposed to be client and contractor; and this was meant to be a debriefing meeting. Discussing business over dinner in a public place was one thing; talking in the privacy of his home was quite another. It felt more like a date.

Maybe she should suggest meeting at the brasserie, instead.

Or maybe she was overthinking things. She shook herself. Of course it wasn't a date. It was work. It was going to be just fine.

In the evening, she headed for his house.

Butterflies were doing a stampede in her stomach by the time she left the Tube station at Paddington. The last time she'd gone to Josh's flat, her world had fallen apart.

She reminded herself that they were both older and wiser, now. Different people. And it wasn't the same situation as before; she wasn't trying to be a knight in shining armour, arriving unannounced on his doorstep. Josh had asked her over for dinner; he was expecting her, and they were planning to discuss business. Everything would be just fine.

And thankfully it wasn't the same place. She didn't think she could've handled meeting him in his Bloomsbury flat. Not with all the memories of that night.

Bayswater was beautiful. When she turned into the cobbled street, she noticed that the mews houses on both sides of the street had terracotta pots and wooden planters stuffed with herbs and flowers outside, everything from geraniums to pansies to bay trees. Some of the houses had wrought-iron Juliet balconies, which were filled with pots of flowers.

There were no cars anywhere; Livi assumed they were parked in the next street at the back of the houses. Some of the houses were painted cream, while others had pale yellow unadorned London brickwork. The ground floors all had the hallmark large double doors of a mews, along with windows containing a dozen smaller panes. The windows were mainly painted white, while the doors were painted heritage colours.

Josh's front door was painted a soft sage green. She rang the doorbell; a few moments later, he opened the door and smiled at her. 'Hello.'

'Your street's so pretty,' she said. 'I totally get why you fell for the location.'

He looked pleased. 'My neighbours are all good sorts. And the local shops are fabulous—everything you could want is within walking distance, and the coffee shop round the corner even roasts its own beans. The only thing missing is a chocolate shop.'

'Hmm. That could be a potential offshoot of Lambert's,' she said with a smile. 'And, speaking of chocolates…' She handed him the bottle of wine she'd bought earlier and a box of chocolates. 'I made them this afternoon.'

'That's very kind, but you really didn't have to bring anything,' he said.

'You know perfectly well that's how Eti and I were brought up,' she said. 'So just shut up and accept everything gracefully, will you?'

'You even sound like your brother,' he teased. 'But thank you. Come in.'

Livi stepped into the small hallway.

'The cloakroom's here, if you need it,' he said, gesturing to a door, then led her through to the doorway opposite into a large all-in-one kitchen, living room and dining room.

The soft sage green of the front door was echoed in the kitchen area, with its sage green cabinets and cream marble worktops. Vegetables were cooking in an electric steamer, and through the glass door of the oven she could see a wrapped foil parcel as well as what looked like vine tomatoes roasting in a tin. The flooring in the kitchen area was terracotta-coloured tile; the rest of the flooring in the room was all polished pale oak, and there was a large cream rug set between the chesterfield sofas in sage green velvet. Clearly that shade of green was one of his favourites, because the curtains were in a pattern she recognised as William Morris's Willow Bough. There were some abstract prints on the walls, and lots of books on the shelves.

And all of a sudden, Livi was very aware that they were alone. Just the two of them. She'd dressed up a bit, for once, actually wearing a little black dress instead of her favourite black trousers, teaming it with heeled shoes she could walk in. Josh had dressed down from the suit he'd worn in the office: a crisp white shirt and faded jeans. The casual look made him more approachable—worse still, *touchable*. And once that thought was in her head, she couldn't shift it.

Which meant she was in trouble.

She wasn't supposed to let herself feel attracted to Josh again. Even if he *had* changed.

'Can I be nosey?' she asked, indicating his bookshelves. It would be an excuse to put a little distance between them, and perhaps then she could get this sudden surge of desire under control.

'Sure. Let me get you a drink?' he said. 'Glass of wine?'

'That'd be lovely,' she said.

He went over to the fridge while she scanned the shelves. There were a few volumes of poetry and classic novels, plus a complete Terry Pratchett collection that didn't surprise her because her brother loved the author, too; but she was a bit surprised to see that there was nothing remotely connected to music. No biographies, and definitely no music scores. She wondered if he'd left them all with his parents so he didn't have to face the memories, or whether he'd given everything away once he'd decided to cut himself off completely from music.

He came back over carrying two glasses of perfectly chilled rosé wine and handed one to her. Livi felt a zing of energy as his skin brushed against hers and nearly dropped the glass. Oh, for pity's sake. She wasn't a teenager anymore, or even the naïve twenty-year-old she'd been that night…

And she wished she hadn't thought of that night. The problem was, she could still remember what it felt like when he'd kissed her. And there was a very big bit of her that wanted to feel it again—because the Josh she'd got to know over the last couple of weeks was more like Dream Josh had always been. A decent guy. Funny, clever. Thoughtful. Someone she would enjoy sharing her life with.

Either he was being tactful or—she hoped—the tangled mess of her feelings didn't show in her face, because he clinked his glass against hers. 'Cheers.'

She took a sip to give herself some breathing space. 'This is gorgeous. Very smooth.'

'From the wine shop round the corner,' he said. 'Sancerre rosé. I thought it would go well with the salmon.'

'That's a good pairing,' she said.

'I like it,' he said, 'but obviously you know more than I do about pairings.'

That sounded almost like an admission that he was actually nervous about cooking for her, despite his bravado yesterday. She smiled. 'I'm not going to grade you out of ten, like some snooty TV chef,' she said. 'It's actually quite nice for someone to make the effort of cooking for me and thinking about the wine. I appreciate it.'

He smiled back. 'Did you ever apply for that TV baking show?'

Of course she hadn't. It had been an excuse to come over to see him. Her stupid attempt to try and help him. He'd noticed her, all right, just as she'd hoped he would. He'd kissed her. Made love with her.

And then there had been the fallout.

Unable to push a single word from her suddenly dry mouth, Livi simply shook her head.

'You really should've given it a go,' he said. 'Everyone in the office was raving about your cakes today. Half of them suggested telling you that they couldn't fill in their questionnaire unless you came back with more, to remind them about what they'd tasted. And they didn't mean just once: they wanted every day for the next month!'

'I guess that's a compliment,' she said.

'Yes. And very much deserved,' he said.

'Thank you.' She inclined her head in acknowledgement of the compliment, but she felt awkward. Time to change the subject. Fast. 'What do you do when you're not at work?' she asked.

'I walk—I'm not far from Hyde Park,' he reminded her. He gestured to the shelves. 'And, as you can see, I read.'

'I was surprised not to see anything even vaguely musical on your bookshelves,' she said. 'Have you really cut yourself off from that world completely?'

'Yes. I don't want to think about anything classical,' he said, 'or at least anything that I would've played, either on the violin or on the piano.'

Livi had noticed the absence of musical instruments or any kind of music system, too. She waited, giving him the chance to fill the silence.

Eventually Josh said, 'I know this is going to sound weird, but I think when you play an instrument you listen to music in slightly a different way to someone who doesn't play. You *feel* it as well as hear it. It's muscle memory, I guess—the same way that a ballet dancer would hear *Swan Lake* but they'd know how it feels to perform it. A musician feels music in their hands. You can't detach one from the other.'

'That makes an odd kind of sense,' she said. 'What about the kind of music you didn't play—say, pop and rock? Do you listen to that?'

'Not really. If I listened to anything, it'd probably be the blues,' he said. 'Though I haven't been to a gig in years.'

'There's nothing like singing your head off with fifty thousand people,' she said. 'I've been to a couple of big gigs with friends at Wembley and Hyde Park and loved every second. And to the Pr—' She stopped mid-sentence, aghast at what she'd just been about to blurt out. Although she hadn't meant to be cruel, saying it would definitely hurt him, and that wasn't who she was. 'Sorry. Ignore me.'

'I'm glad people still enjoy the Proms,' he said, clearly picking up what she hadn't said.

Well, she'd brought up the subject and he hadn't shied away from it. Maybe she could push a little more, after all. 'You played a couple of Proms, didn't you?'

He nodded. 'I did the *Lark*, and the Paganini *Caprice*.'

'I saw you play the *Lark*,' she said softly. 'At St Martin's, and at the Royal Albert Hall. The first time, I looked up Meredith's poem when I got home, and what I read…that was exactly what you made me see.'

'"He rises and begins to round, /He drops the silver chain of sound/ Of many links without a break, /In chirrup, whistle, slur and shake,"' Josh quoted. 'Vaughan Williams wrote some of that poem in his score.'

'The bit I remember most is, "And ever winging up and up,/ Our valley is his golden cup, /And he the wine which overflows /To lift us with him as he goes",' she said. 'That's what I saw in my mind's eye when you played. A skylark rising into the air, the melody dropping down to us and taking us up with him.' She looked at him. 'Josh, it must be incredibly tough to know you can't play it anymore. But nobody can deny the joy you've brought to your audiences when you were able to play. The joy you still bring, because there are recordings of your work and people can still play them. That's special. Something to hold on to.'

'Maybe I'm being a bit self-indulgent,' he said.

'No. You're protecting yourself,' she said. 'I

get that. But have you ever thought that cutting yourself off from the joy of music might hurt you more? Even though you can't play it, you can still feel it in your heart.'

Josh wasn't sure he even had a heart, these days. He kept it well covered, thinking he was protecting himself; or maybe a closed-up heart just turned to stone from lack of use. 'Maybe,' he said.

She reached out and squeezed his hand briefly. 'You asked me a few days ago what I'd do if I couldn't cook anymore—if the only thing I could do was boil an egg, with a lot of help, would I do that? I told you I wouldn't, because I completely understand why you don't want to play at anything less than the level you played at before. But there's a difference between being a creator and being a consumer. I'd still eat.'

'You kind of *have* to eat, if you want to stay alive,' he pointed out dryly.

'You need to consume enough calories to make your body function and make sure you get all the nutrients you need,' she said, 'but there's a big difference in seeing food solely as fuel, and enjoying what you eat for its own sake—being able to savour the taste and the texture, the scent, the way it looks. If I couldn't cook, I'd still enjoy the food. Maybe I'd find patisserie a bit difficult to manage, but if it was a choice between not having it in my life at all and having it in my life in just a little way…' She spread her hands. 'Well, I'd want to keep it in my life. I'd want to keep at least some of the joy.'

She had a point, but Josh didn't want to think about that. Instead, he switched topic. 'What do you do when you're not working?'

'I work unsocial hours,' she said, 'so it's either the cinema or theatre on my nights off, or maybe a matinée performance. And I like wandering around art galleries.' She smiled. 'Holly, my best friend, is really good at craft stuff. She knits, she sews and she crochets.'

'The history teacher, right?' he asked.

She looked pleased that he'd paid attention. 'Yes. She did try to teach me to knit, because she says it's great for relaxation, but my scarf ended up more holes than knitting, and it was a very peculiar shape.' She chuckled. 'So we gave up. The deal is that she knits me a gorgeous cardigan for winter, and I make her a batch of cake every week when I'm trying new ideas.'

'You bake on your days off?' He'd known

Livi was driven, but he hadn't realised how much: that she continued working even when she wasn't in the brasserie.

'It's not really work. I play with recipes,' she said. 'Ideas. Sometimes they work, sometimes they don't. But you never know until you try.' She paused. 'I'm going to Brussels in a couple of weeks, for a chocolatier's course.'

'If you need guinea pigs,' he said, 'I can supply a few.'

She chuckled. 'Speaking of which, I need to earn my supper. I got your report this morning. Shall we sit down and talk about it?'

He glanced at his watch. 'Dinner's just about ready. Let's do it over coffee.'

Do it. He felt colour scorch into his face. Oh, for pity's sake. Way to go, Josh, he thought. How to make her feel uncomfortable around him. 'Analyse the questionnaires, I mean,' he mumbled.

'Anything I can do to help with dinner?'

'No. Come and sit down,' he said, ushering her to the table.

He'd chosen recipes for their simplicity, remembering what she'd said about simple food. Baked salmon, roasted vine tomatoes, steamed Jersey Royal potatoes with a little butter, and asparagus wrapped in prosciutto and baked with a little parmesan scattered on top.

'This,' she said appreciatively, 'goes together really well. And you've plated it very nicely.' She looked up at him, the corners of her eyes crinkling with mischief. 'It'd get you a pretty good mark at chef school.'

He couldn't help laughing, 'Well, you said to keep it simple.'

'It's the principle my dad brought me up on,' she said. 'Good food doesn't need extra complications. Just use good quality ingredients, keep the preparation simple, and let the food shine in its own right.'

'That's a good rule for life,' he said. 'Be honest. Be yourself.' Something he maybe hadn't been since the accident, because he still had that gaping hole in his centre. He'd learned to cover it up, but it was still there. And he hadn't ever told the people closest to him what he'd nearly done, that awful night. He'd wanted to protect them from the knowledge, because he didn't want to hurt them by telling them the truth; but keeping a secret also meant he'd ended up keeping a space between himself and the people he loved. And sometimes he really missed how it felt to be close to someone.

'Be yourself. That works for me,' she said lightly. As if she guessed that he was feeling awkward and a bit out of sorts, she switched the topic of conversation, talking about recent films she'd enjoyed, and Josh found himself relaxing again with her.

Olivia Lambert really was like balm to the soul. Did she realise how special she was? he wondered. And would she give him that second chance, if he asked her to?

Over coffee, they went through the questionnaire results.

'The menu's in the right area,' she said. 'And I like the suggestions of us offering picnic boxes and takeaway lunches. It'd work if we open a café, but I think it would be too much to add it to the brasserie.'

'I'd advise a soft launch in the brasserie,' Josh said. 'Cake of the day on your socials, reviews on the foodie sites—including Jenna's vegan one—film of you making something, and running a competition to see if they can guess the flavour, that sort of thing. Focus on your Belgian heritage, use old family photos of the brasserie when your family first started out in London, and if there's anything of you as a toddler making cakes with your mum or your gran we can use them. Those sort of things, with the personal touch, go down really well. Your brand's all about family, good home cooking and the Belgian twist on things.'

'That's all doable,' she said. 'I've definitely got film of toddler me making cakes with Gran.'

'We can do it as a reel,' he said. 'You as a toddler, you as a teenager, you doing the patisserie course, graduation. We want customers—young and old—talking about their favourite cake and their favourite tartine. Give me the material, and we'll sort it out for you.'

'All right,' she said. 'Let's make a list of what you need.'

When they were done, she sent the list over to him. 'Just in case you have any bright ideas tomorrow,' she said with a smile. 'And I need to be getting back.'

For work. From what she'd told him, he was pretty sure she started early and finished late. 'Of course,' he said. 'I'll walk you back to the Tube.'

'No need. It's still light,' she said. 'I'll be fine. And I'm sure you have things to do. Can I do the washing up, first?'

'No. That's what dishwashers are for,' he said.

'Thank you for dinner,' she said. 'I really enjoyed it.'

'Thank you for the wine and the chocolates,' he said. 'I'm keeping that quiet at work, or they'll all come round to raid my fridge.'

She chuckled. 'I'll drop some of the next batch round.' Then, to his surprise, at his front door, she rose on tiptoes and pressed a kiss on his cheek. 'I'll speak to you soon,' she said, and sashayed out of the door.

He didn't recognise the light scent she wore—oranges and toffee, he thought, and something he couldn't quite work out that felt sparkly—but it put him in a spin. Or maybe that had been the feel of her mouth against his skin. He watched her walking down the cobbled street, hoping she'd look back at him when she reached the corner and feeling ridiculously disappointed when she didn't. He closed the door and touched his cheek, tracing the outline her lips had made. This was crazy. He wasn't supposed to be feeling like this about her. She was his client, which put her off limits; and that night, years ago, put her even more off limits. But, even knowing that, the more time he spent with her, the more he wanted to be with her.

They'd become friends again, of a sort.

He wanted a lot more than friendship from her; but, until he knew how Livi felt, he needed to keep his own feelings under wraps. Rushing things now would ruin everything. He just needed to wait. Be patient. Be professional. And, most of all, keep that need under strict control.

CHAPTER SEVEN

EITHER LIVI WAS rushed off her feet at the brasserie, or she'd decided to put some space between them, Josh thought, because she kept everything strictly on business terms for the next week.

Then, on the Monday morning, she sent him a text. Wanna be a guinea pig?

He remembered the afternoon tea she'd brought over, the previous week—the team was still raving about it. Me, or the team? he checked.

Just you.

Sure, he said, trying to play it cool. When were you thinking?

Dinner tonight at seven, she said. My place. Make sure you're hungry.

Oh, dear God, the pictures that put in his head. He rather thought he needed a cold shower. Look forward to it, he said. Flat above the restaurant, yes?

Red door next to it. Press the intercom for Flat One.

OK. Shall I bring red, white or rosé wine? he asked.

Whatever you'd like to drink with chicken, she replied.

He found it hard to concentrate all afternoon. And clearly it showed, because his team kept making little comments and asking what had put him in such a good mood.

No way could he tell them. He made some bland excuse.

But even the idea of seeing Olivia Lambert again made him feel like a teenager.

This wasn't a proper date. 'Guinea pig' meant that she was testing something out on him. Probably brunch, he thought. He needed to think of this as work.

But he couldn't.

She'd said he could bring wine. And she'd liked the rosé Sancerre. He couldn't take her chocolates—especially as he knew she was going to Brussels on Friday for a chocolatier's course. But he could take flowers.

Roses were too obvious.

And a big flashy bouquet would make her run a mile.

In the end, he went to the florist round the corner at lunchtime and asked for help. 'I need something that isn't too obvious or too flashy, but it's for someone…' He paused. 'Someone special to me.'

'Do they have a favourite flower?' the florist asked.

'Um—I don't know,' he said.

'OK. Let's try a different tack. Do you know what colours they like?' the florist asked.

'No.' And how bad was it that he'd known her for twenty-five years—well, with a bit of a gap, and he'd only got to know the woman she was now over the last three weeks—and he didn't have the faintest clue? 'Sorry. Um, if it helps, she's a pastry chef.'

The florist smiled. 'Actually, that does help. We'll go for a summery scent. Stocks would be good.'

'She likes gardens,' he said, brightening up.

'All right. I can do you a hatbox arrangement, so you won't have to worry about whether she has the right size vase. Stocks, chrysanthemums—the tiny santini ones are really pretty—irises and alstroemeria,' the florist suggested. 'Pink, cream and blue. We can add in some cream roses, too; as part of a mixed bouquet, they add depth and they're not obvious.' She smiled. 'A bit nicer than a dozen red roses, and it'll be special but not completely over the top.'

Which fitted his brief exactly. 'Perfect. Thank you,' Josh said.

He collected the flowers later that afternoon, finished off some work at home, then took a cab to Covent Garden. He went to the red door next to the restaurant and pressed the intercom for Flat One; there was an answering buzz, and a click as the door opened.

On the landing at the top of the first flight of stairs, Livi stood at the open door. 'Good evening. Perfect timing.'

He handed her the wine and the flowers.

'Oh, these are so lovely!' she said. 'How did you know stocks were my favourite flowers?'

'I didn't,' he admitted. 'I asked the florist for something nice that someone who loves gardens would like. I mean—I could hardly bring a box of chocolates to a chocolatier, could I?'

She chuckled. 'You have a point. They're stunning.' She buried her face in the flowers for a moment, inhaling their scent. 'Thank you. Come in and sit down.'

He closed the door behind him, and she indicated the middle doorway. 'The bathroom's there, if you need it.'

He assumed the first door was her bedroom. When he followed her through the third door into the open-plan kitchen-cum-living room, he stopped dead. 'Wow. I wasn't expecting *this*,' he said, glancing round. The walls were painted a deep grey-blue, and the matt colour extended to the kitchen cabinets. The counter-tops and splashback were cream marble, and there was a white marble fireplace surround; there was an ornamental metal basket piled with logs in the fireplace itself. The two sash windows had roman blinds in what looked to him like a Morris pattern; there was a rich crimson-and-white rug in the centre of the polished floorboards, and a comfortable-looking sofa in crimson velvet with matching tub chairs by the windows. There was a brass and crystal chandelier hanging from the ceiling, reflected in the mirror above the fireplace. There were bookshelves—painted in the same matt colour as the kitchen cabinets—and he could see at a glance that they contained mainly classic novels and poetry.

'I'm going to put these here,' she said, placing the flowers on the occasional table between the chairs. 'And how clever of you to get them in a hatbox so I don't have to rummage around for a vase.'

'I can't take credit for that. It was the florist's suggestion,' he admitted.

'But you were sensible enough to take it,' she pointed out.

He didn't feel very sensible, right now. He felt all at sixes and sevens. 'Your flat is amazing,' he said. 'And it's a really bold colour choice. Most heritage places tend to be painted cream, to make the most of the light.'

'Covent Garden deserves something theatrical,' she said with a grin. 'I admit, the flat was painted cream when I moved in—some of the wall in my bedroom is actually bare brick. Holly's cousin was training as an interior designer and asked if she could redesign the flat for me as part of her degree project. I said yes—and I admit, I panicked a bit when she brought the paint round because I thought it'd be way too dark and I'd feel as if I were living in a rabbit warren. But she asked me to trust her, painted the whole flat the same colour—including all the woodwork—and I love it.'

The small round dining table was set for two, with a white damask tablecloth and napkins folded into a rose shape, silver cutlery and plain crystal wine glasses.

And something smelled incredible.

'Anything I can do to help?' he asked.

'You can open the wine and pour two glasses, if you like, then sit down,' she said. 'I'm just about ready to serve up.'

He followed her directions, and she dished up.

'It's chicken breast stuffed with goat's cheese and sundried tomatoes, and wrapped in parma ham, served on a bed of puy lentils and spinach with a pesto dressing,' she said. 'And the bread's sourdough.'

It had taken her seconds to add the little fancy finishing touches that he never even thought about using when he was cooking, but which made the food look special. And the food tasted every bit as good as it looked. Even though she was a pastry specialist, she could hold her own when it came to cooking the other courses.

She wouldn't so much as let him clear the table for her when they'd finished the main course. 'It's fine,' she said with a smile.

And then she brought out the pudding: a small dome with a deep raspberry-coloured mirror glaze, topped with a stylised daisy made from white chocolate.

He'd known she was talented, but this went beyond his expectations.

'That looks incredible.' He blinked. 'I'm almost scared to touch it in case I spoil it.'

She laughed. 'It's not for decoration, it's for eating. It's a white chocolate and raspberry mousse with a raspberry gelée, on an almond sponge, with a raspberry mirror glaze. If you slice through it with your spoon, you'll see the layers properly.'

'Just… I knew you were a proper *pâtissière*, and Eti always raves about your desserts,' he said, 'but I wasn't expecting something like this.'

She chuckled. 'I admit this was a bit time-consuming to make—you have to freeze the layers as you go, and obviously with this being raspberry I needed to do a bit of sieving as well, to take out the pips. I didn't have time to make them when I did the afternoon tea at your office, but here I could take my time. Technically, it's known as an *entremet*.'

He picked up his spoon and sliced into the dome so he could see the layers, the pale sponge and the dark gelée and the fluffy pale pink mousse and the glaze. And then he hesitated. 'This is going to be part of the afternoon tea?'

'Some days,' she said. 'I've done a blueberry version before now, and a passion fruit and orange one which looks almost fluorescent.'

He narrowed his eyes at her. 'This isn't greed speaking—well, it might be that as well—but did you only make two of them?'

She smiled. 'No. I have several more in the fridge.'

'Good. If you don't mind, I'll ask Pete to nip round to the brasserie and photograph them tomorrow,' he said. 'Because I guarantee that pictures of this pudding alone will get people to queue up in the brasserie for your afternoon tea.'

She looked pleased. 'Good. But the proof of the pudding is meant to be in the *eating*.'

He took the hint and tried the first spoonful, then closed his eyes in bliss. And all the common sense went flying out of his head, because he found himself saying, 'I think you should call this First Kiss. That's what it's like—light and sweet, but not cloying, and it makes you want more.'

First kiss.

Their own first kiss hadn't been light or sweet, Livi thought. It had been hot and needy and desperate. And it had led to disaster. To recriminations and misery.

But maybe, just maybe, this was a second chance.

A first kiss that was light and sweet…

She'd impulsively kissed Josh on the cheek, last week, but he hadn't mentioned it again. She'd thought he was being polite and ignoring the subject to avoid embarrassment, so she'd backed off. But the way he'd blurted out the words, just now, made her wonder if he'd been thinking the same thing that she had, all along.

His eyes were still closed, and his lips were very slightly parted—just a tiny, tiny gap in the centre. A wave of sheer heat throbbed through her. Right at that second, he looked as sexy as sin. Irresistible.

Before she knew what she was doing, she stood up, closed the gap between them in two steps, bent down and brushed her mouth against his.

First kiss.

Light and sweet, but not cloying.

Makes you want more.

And that tiny contact between them, that gossamer whisper of a kiss, had made her lips tingle. She wanted more.

He opened his eyes, then; they were like deep blue pools, reflecting the same need and longing that burned through her.

'Livi,' he whispered, and reached up to brush her cheek with the backs of his fingers. And then he shifted and scooped her onto his lap, holding her close. She slid her arms round his neck to balance herself, and he reached up so his mouth just brushed hers. Tiny, tiny kisses, little butterfly movements, and it felt like fireworks going off in her head. All she could see was glittering stars.

This was the kiss she'd wanted all those years ago. The kiss in her head that nobody had ever matched up to, before. Yet Josh was kissing her now, kissing her properly, and it was perfect. It was *everything.*

Josh.

Josh, who'd pushed her away and stomped on her heart.

Josh.

She couldn't do this. Panic flooded through her. Last time, it had all gone wrong. And OK, now it was years later and they'd both grown up and changed, but what was to say that this time wasn't a mistake, too? What was to say that he wouldn't let her down again?

Clearly he felt the tension that had made her freeze, because he stopped kissing her.

'Livi,' he said softly.

How could she face him?

What if she saw rejection in his eyes again?

How could she have been so *stupid*, when they were supposed to be working together and being professional and, and, and…

'Breathe, Livi,' he said quietly, taking her hand and squeezing it.

Oh, God. She'd panicked so much that she'd actually stopped breathing. 'I…'

'Don't talk. Breathe with me. In for four,' he said softly. 'Out for four.'

It was easier to give in and follow his directions. Though even after several breaths she still felt light-headed, and she thought that was more than just down to breathing: it was his nearness. The fact his arms were still round her. The fact those blue eyes were filled with concern. And oh, dear God, he was so damned sexy and she wanted him so much, she didn't know what to do with herself.

'Livi.' He kissed the tip of her nose. 'We need to talk. Properly. But I think you need some space, first, so I'm going to leave now. I'll call you tomorrow.'

Meaning he'd talk to her later, after he'd found a kind way to tell her he wasn't interested—that as far as he was concerned she was still Eti's baby sister? Which meant that this *was* just the same as the last time he'd rejected her, except this time he'd have a veneer of kindness instead of bitter scornfulness when he told her that he didn't want her—that he couldn't want someone like her, and she'd never be what he wanted.

Misery welled up in her heart.

'Tomorrow,' he said softly. He stood up, still holding her, then settled her gently into the chair he'd just vacated. The chair that was still warm with his body heat. Ridiculously, she felt freezing cold.

He pressed the backs of his fingers briefly against her cheek in a gesture of affection, then left the room. She heard the click of her front door as it closed behind him.

What the hell was she going to do now?

CHAPTER EIGHT

TIME SEEMED TO STOP. Livi wasn't sure if it was seconds or minutes or even longer until she finally forced herself to move and clear up in the kitchen.

A warm shower did nothing to relax her. Neither did listening to music, because music made her think of Josh. And she couldn't concentrate enough to read or even watch a re-run of an old favourite sitcom.

What was she going to do?

She didn't want to fall for Josh and for him to let her down again.

Kissing him had been a huge mistake. A whim she should never, ever have acted upon. Maybe it had been a mixture of proximity and unfinished business; but she couldn't get it out of her head, and it rattled her. Over the last three weeks, she'd discovered that she really liked the man Josh had become. Was she still in love with Josh, after all these years? Was that the real reason why she'd never managed to get a relationship to work—because the men she'd dated hadn't been *him*?

She spent a sleepless night and was seriously out of sorts, the next morning. Josh had said he'd talk to her later today, but she didn't have a clue what she was going to say to him. Worst of all, she still had some of the raspberry *entremets* in her fridge—the 'first kiss', as Josh had dubbed them—and she knew he was planning to send his photographer over to shoot them.

Livi really couldn't face dealing with that, pretending that everything was fine when it wasn't.

Even though Tuesday was usually her day off, she boxed up the desserts and headed down to the brasserie. Maybe the photographer could shoot the *entremets* in the kitchen, rather than in her flat. And maybe doing an extra shift, keeping herself too busy to think about what had happened with Josh, would help to clear her head. At least it would be doing something practical instead of moping around her flat, full of angst.

'Hello, sweetheart. I wasn't expecting to see you today,' Sophie said, when Livi walked into the kitchen.

'Josh is sending a photographer over, this morning, to shoot these for some social media posts,' Livi said, gesturing to the box.

Sophie took a look inside. 'That mirror glaze looks amazing—and I like that chocolate daisy. Raspberry, I'd guess?'

'Raspberry and white chocolate layers, on a bed of almond sponge,' Livi confirmed. 'Once they've been photographed, they're up for grabs if you and Dad want to try one.'

Sophie's eyes narrowed and Livi knew that her mum had picked up on the flatness of her voice, even though she'd tried to hide it.

'Is everything all right, darling?' Sophie asked quietly.

'Yes,' Livi said. Then, knowing that her mum would see straight through the fib, she admitted, 'No.' She sighed. 'I don't know, Mum.'

'That sounds…complicated.'

Sophie sounded warm and non-judgemental, and Livi wanted to throw herself into her mum's arms and burst into tears. Except that wasn't who she was. Olivia Lambert was cool, calm and sensible…or she had been, until Josh Garrett had come back into her life. Right now, she was a hot mess, and she hated feeling so out of control. 'It is.'

'Talk to me, sweetheart,' Sophie said. 'Whatever it is, we can sort it out.'

'I'm not sure we can.' Livi bit her lip. 'I've made a really stupid mistake.'

Sophie waited, giving her space, and eventually Livi burst out, 'I kissed Josh, last night.'

'I think that was rather a long time coming,' Sophie said neutrally.

Livi laughed wryly. 'Mum, if you only knew.'

'Tell me,' Sophie said gently.

Livi glanced round the busy kitchen. Much as she liked her team, she didn't want to bare her soul in front of them. 'Not here.'

'The office, then. Your dad's out at a supplier's.' Sophie deftly grabbed two mugs on the way out of the kitchen, filled them with filter coffee and thrust one into Livi's hands when they reached the office and Livi sat down. 'Take a big gulp, then talk.'

The coffee didn't help at all, but Livi supposed at least the mug gave her something to do with her hands. 'It started years ago.' She told Sophie what had happened the night she'd gone to rescue Josh.

Sophie leaned over, took the mug from her daughter's hand and placed it on the desk next to her own, and held Livi close. 'Oh, darling. I'm so sorry I didn't know any of this, back then. And you've been carrying the burden ever since? I wish you'd told me. I could've helped you deal with it.'

Livi shook her head. 'I couldn't tell you, Mum. I was just so *ashamed*.'

'You did nothing wrong. Josh, on the other hand, most definitely did,' Sophie said grimly.

Livi winced. 'He was in a pretty bad place at the time.'

'You're protecting him, after what he said?' Sophie looked shocked.

'It did hurt me, the way he pushed me away afterwards. How he dismissed me as a stupid, spotty-faced schoolgirl.' She took a deep breath. 'It hurt so much.' And the comment about her skin had stung viciously. Like anyone else who'd ever suffered from teenage spots that hung around a bit longer than the teens, she'd been sensitive about the way she looked.

'Of course it hurt. It was a horrible thing to do. And you were never a stupid schoolgirl. Even when you were at school, you were never immature. And as for that thing about your skin, I could punch him for being so tactless. You were still growing up, for pity's sake.' Sophie looked furious. 'I know he'd just had a life-altering injury, but it sounds to me as if he knew you had a crush on him and he deliberately broke your heart, so someone else would feel as bad as he did.' Sophie hadn't taken her arms from round her daughter, and Livi could feel the tension in her mum's body. 'Right now, I could happily break every bone in that man's body.'

Sophie looked at her sweet, lovely mother—the woman who made people feel the brightness in life—and shook her head. 'That's not who you are, Mum. And I rather think he's beaten himself up about it enough ever since.' She rested her forehead against her mum's shoulder. 'He wrote to me, a few weeks afterwards.'

'And he apologised?'

'So he says. I never actually read the letter.' She took a deep breath. 'I didn't throw it away, either.' Though she wasn't sure why. She should have shredded it. Burned it. Done something with it, instead of leaving it as a ticking time-bomb. 'It's upstairs at the back of a drawer somewhere.' That wasn't quite true; she knew exactly where the letter was. She just hadn't had the courage to read it. Even now. Because giving her virginity to Joshua Garrett had *meant* something to her; she didn't want to read something that dismissed it as a mistake.

'Maybe it's time you did read it,' Sophie said.

'I don't think I'm ready for that,' Livi admitted. She raked a hand through her hair. 'I don't know what to do, Mum. Right now, I just want to run away, but that's not fair to you.'

'You're on that chocolatier course in Brussels in two days' time,' Sophie said. 'Why don't you go early and give yourself a bit of space? And don't worry about cover here. It's only a couple of days. I'll sort it out.' She paused. 'Do you want me to come with you?'

Yes, but Livi knew that would put the rest of the team under too much pressure and that wouldn't be fair. She couldn't even ask Holly to come with her for a couple of days, because she was in Greece with her boyfriend. 'I think I need to be alone,' she fibbed. 'Like you say, I need some space. To think.'

'All right, but you know you can call me any time. And you can change your mind. Text me if you need me there, and I'll be on the next train or plane to Brussels.' Sophie stroked her hair. 'I'd even drive over through the Channel Tunnel, if I had to.' Which Livi knew was a huge ask, because her mum hated driving abroad.

Livi believed her. Sophie had always had her back, and Eti's. 'I love you, Mum.'

'I love you, too, my precious girl.' Sophie hugged her.

'Don't break Josh's bones,' Livi said.

'I'll hold off until you're back home and you've sorted your head out,' Sophie said. 'That's as far as I'm prepared to promise. Now, go upstairs and finish packing. I'll change your hotel booking and your train tickets.'

'And don't tell Dad?'

Sophie looked troubled. 'I've never kept anything from your dad.'

'Please. Just until I'm back,' Livi said. 'I'd rather tell him myself. But I can't face doing that today.'

'All right,' Sophie said. 'As long as you promise me you'll call if you need me.'

'I will,' Livi promised. 'And thank you. For understanding.'

'Of course I understand. You were twenty years old. It didn't feel like a crush. You were in love with him, and he took advantage of that. And then he broke your heart.'

'I was the one who kissed him, last night.'

Hot shame flooded through Livi's veins. 'Then he left.'

'Oh, darling.' Sophie stroked her hair. 'You can't help who you fall for. But if he doesn't treat you the way you deserve to be treated, you're better off without him. And if it's too difficult for you to work with him, then we'll pay off the contract and use someone else.'

'He said he'd talk to me today. But I can't face him.' Livi grimaced. 'Right now, I feel embarrassed and stupid and clumsy.'

'You're neither stupid nor clumsy,' Sophie said briskly. 'Or you wouldn't be about to take over the reins of the brasserie and move the business forward. But maybe it's a little tricky to mix business and...well, emotional stuff. Try not to worry. It'll all come out in the wash, as my gran used to say.'

Livi smiled wryly. 'I guess.'

Sophie gave her a last squeeze. 'Go and pack. A bit of distance will give you some perspective. And this is about what *you* want. Whatever you decide that is, you have my full backing.'

'Even if I decide I want Josh?' Livi tested.

'Whatever you decide. Just know that your father and I love you very much, and we're hugely proud of you,' Sophie said.

'I love you both, too,' Livi said.

And that chat with her mum made her feel better enough that she could pack swiftly.

She glanced at the flowers in her living room before she left her flat, and on impulse grabbed them and took them down to the brasserie.

'Darling, they're utterly gorgeous, but I'm your mum and it's my job to be there for you and listen when you're having a tough time. You really didn't need to rush out and get me flowers,' Sophie said.

'I didn't,' Livi admitted. 'Actually, Josh brought me these, last night. And they're so lovely. I'd rather give them to you so you can enjoy them than leave them in my flat and let them shrivel unseen while I'm away.'

'Then I'm the lucky one,' Sophie said lightly. She paused. 'They really are gorgeous.'

'He said he couldn't bring chocolates to a chocolatier,' Livi said. 'But these…'

'…are quite a bit more special than the average supermarket bouquet,' Sophie finished. 'And they're not the sort of flowers you give to any old someone. It looks to me as if Josh might have feelings for you.'

Livi had thought that, too. But had she been deluding herself, seeing something that wasn't really there? 'What if he changes his mind? What if he thinks it's a mistake? I mean, *I* worry it might have been a mistake.'

'Distance and perspective—that's what you need,' Sophie said. 'Think about what *you* want. Then you'll be in a place to have a proper conversation with him.'

Livi smiled wryly. 'That's common sense, and I should've worked that out for myself.'

'It's a lot easier to do from the outside, when you're not the one tying yourself in knots,' Sophie said. 'Go to Brussels. Make chocolate. Sit in the sun drinking good coffee and eating waffles. Go to art galleries. Let your subconscious work it out for you.' She glanced at her watch. 'You have a train to catch. Go. Safe journey. I love you.'

'Love you, too, Mum,' Livi said. 'I'll ring you when I get to the hotel.'

Josh frowned. Livi wasn't responding to emails or texts, and when he rang her phone it went straight to voicemail.

Had she had second thoughts after he'd left her flat last night, and was trying to avoid him now? Or maybe he was being paranoid. Hadn't she said that she sometimes swapped her shifts if they were short-staffed at the brasserie? If she was working, then she probably wouldn't have her phone with her.

He still needed the photographs of her amazing desserts as part of the social media campaign. He probably should've taken the shots last night, instead of kissing her back. That had been mistake number one. Mistake number two had been kissing her back.

And mistake number three had been leaving.

Or had it?

The very first time he'd kissed her, he'd rushed her. He'd taken everything she'd offered. And then he'd panicked, and said things that he knew would push her away. Things that had hurt her badly, and even now it made him feel ashamed.

This time round, he'd wanted to get it right. He'd wanted to give her space, to make sure this was really what she wanted and he wasn't railroading her into anything. That was definitely the right thing to do, he was sure.

But it felt as if it had backfired. Had she thought he was walking away from her again, instead of trying to be honourable and letting her dictate the pace rather than his own need?

They needed to talk. He'd been clear about that, last night. He'd told her he'd call her this morning. And surely she'd learned over the last few weeks that she could trust him—that if she could trust him with her family's business, she could trust him with herself?

The quickest way round this, he thought, was go to the brasserie and talk to her. They'd arranged for him to photograph the raspberry *entremets*; instead of sending Peter, he'd do it himself.

At Covent Garden, he rang the intercom for Livi's flat, but there was no answer. That had to mean she was at the brasserie, he decided.

When he walked into Lambert's, Sophie was on front of house. She greeted him with folded arms, a narrow stare and a very cool voice. 'Joshua. Good morning.'

Uh-oh. This didn't sound good.

'Good morning, Sophie,' he said politely. 'I was hoping to talk to Livi and sort out some photographs of her amazing desserts for social media, but I can't get hold of her.'

'She said you were sending a photographer over.'

'I was,' he said, 'but I'm doing it myself so I can talk to her. I assume she's in the kitchen?'

And just like that the curvy, smiling woman he'd known and liked for years turned into a forbidding, granite crag. 'I'm afraid not.'

Sudden fear flooded through him. 'Is she all right?'

'I rather think you should've asked that question eight years ago,' she said quietly and very, very coldly.

Josh stared at her in shock, understanding now why she'd turned glacial on him. 'You *know* about that?'

'I do now,' Sophie said. 'Livi told me this morning.' She narrowed her eyes even further at him. 'My little girl's been hurting all these years, and I didn't have a clue.'

'Sophie, that wasn't your fault. It was mine. And Livi's not a little girl. She's the most amazing woman I've ever met,' Josh said. 'Eight years ago, I was in a bad place—and that's an explanation, not an excuse. I said things I know I shouldn't have said, and I've always regretted hurting her. I've apologised. Since we've been working together recently, I've realised…' He stopped abruptly. 'Actually, with the greatest respect, I need to discuss that with her, not with you.'

'Perhaps,' Sophie said, still unbending. 'I'll let you get on with taking your photographs. Let me show you through to the kitchen.'

Josh wasn't used to his best friend's mother being so cool with him, though he could understand why; now she knew how badly he'd treated Livi, of course she was angry with him.

He needed Sophie on his side, not against him. He didn't want to tell her how he felt about Livi because, although he knew his feelings for Livi were deepening, he wasn't entirely clear yet where this thing between them was going. And although he knew he could tell Sophie Lambert something that would shock her into being on his side, he wasn't ready to open up about *that*, either. To anyone.

Without arguing, he followed Sophie into the kitchen. And he tried not to be disappointed when he discovered that Livi's mum hadn't just been trying to protect her; Livi really wasn't in the kitchen. Then again, if Livi had guessed that he might come to take the photographs himself, she was probably avoiding him.

Even looking at the desserts made him remember the previous night. The way Livi had walked round the table to him and kissed him. How he'd scooped her into his lap and kissed her back. Her warmth. How the world had finally felt as if it had fallen into place instead of being slightly off kilter the whole time.

And he had a pretty good idea of why she'd

fled. She didn't trust him not to let her down again. He could hardly blame her for that. She might even be right, and that was a terrifying proposition.

Planning and strategy were two of his key skills at work, but they completely deserted him where Livi was concerned. How was he going to convince her that he was no longer the broken young violin prodigy who'd let her down so badly? That he'd moved on, sorted himself out, and this time she could rely on him?

Brooding wasn't going to help. He forced himself to be professional and take the photographs of the raspberry *entremets*, firstly the complete dome with its immaculate mirror shine reflecting the white chocolate daisy, and then the cross-section with the utterly precise layers.

'That mirror glaze is incredible,' one of the sous-chefs said as Josh zoomed the camera in and took a shot. 'Our Livi's a marvel.'

'Yes, she is,' Josh agreed.

'I can't wait to see the ideas she'll come back with from Brussels.'

'Her chocolatier course is later this week, isn't it?' Josh asked.

'Yes, but she's gone a couple of days early

to check out desserts, brunch and afternoon tea,' the sous-chef said.

Livi had gone to Brussels already?

That made sense. It would give her some space and time to think.

And maybe Brussels would be a good place for them to talk. Somewhere neutral. No memories, no misunderstandings, no mess of the past.

Which meant he needed to know where she was staying; he could probably find out where the course was, especially as he knew the dates, but it wouldn't be fair to Livi to turn up there.

The one person who could tell him the details probably wouldn't want to help him. But he could try.

Once he'd thanked the kitchen team for letting him sort out the photographs, he went in search of Sophie again.

'Finished?' she asked.

'Almost,' he said. 'Sophie, about that night. I was still coming to terms with things, and not doing a very good job of it.' He'd almost taken a step that would've shattered his family. Not that he was going to open up to Sophie about *that*. 'When I realised what I'd done, and how Livi really felt about me—that she wanted a proper relationship, and my head was in way too much of a mess at the time to even consider doing anything like that—I panicked. That's why I said what I did. To push her away.'

'So I gather,' Sophie said grimly.

'But because I realised how much I'd hurt her, I finally started to sort my life out. I went to therapy. I wrote to Livi, apologising and explaining I didn't actually mean what I'd said to her. When she didn't reply, I assumed she didn't want anything to do with me. I tried to stay out of her way so I wouldn't make life harder for her. If you remember, I ducked out of Eti's wedding and Louisa's christening.' And he would have been so thrilled to be Eti's best man and Louisa's godfather, even though he felt he hadn't deserved that privilege.

'Eti said you'd gone somewhere for residential therapy.'

'I did,' Josh said. 'Strictly speaking, I was managing OK at the time without it, but I needed an excuse that nobody would question and meant that nobody would connect Livi to my absence. I didn't want anyone to blame her or give her a hard time, because none of it was her fault.'

Sophie gave a single nod, signalling that she understood.

'When you gave me the brasserie project and I realised I was going to have to work with Livi, I asked her if she wanted me to back off,' Josh said. 'I said I'd be guided by her. I could turn down the project, or get one of my team to stand in for me, or we could agree to put the past behind us and work together.' He blew out a breath. 'She decided she could trust me to be professional.'

'And she was wrong.'

'No, she wasn't,' Josh said. 'Livi and I need to talk. I know she's in Brussels, and maybe that'd be a good place to meet. Somewhere neutral, away from London and away from the past.' He looked at Sophie. 'Can you tell me which hotel she's staying at, please?'

'Maybe you should give her space,' Sophie said.

'Maybe giving her space means she'll think too much and it'll get blown out of proportion,' he countered. 'I promise you, I'm not going to hurt her again. I just want to talk to her. Face to face—it's too easy to miss things in a video call, and even easier to misinterpret things in a phone call or text messages. But, more than talking to her, I want to listen to her.'

Sophie was silent, as if weighing things up. He waited rather than rushing her. He needed her to be sure he wasn't going to bulldoze her daughter's feelings—and being patient now would prove to her that she could trust him to be patient with Livi, too.

'If I tell you her hotel details,' Sophie said, 'I expect you to book a room somewhere else.'

'Of course,' he agreed. 'I won't crowd her.'

'All right,' she said. 'But I'm telling her that you're heading to Brussels, so she can prepare herself for seeing you again. And if she decides she's not ready to talk to you, Joshua, I expect you to abide by that and wait until she *is* ready.'

Let Livi be the one to decide the pace. Josh didn't even need to think about it before he answered. 'Yes. That's fair,' he said. 'Thank you.'

She took her phone from her pocket. 'It's probably quickest if I email you the booking confirmation.'

'Thank you, Sophie,' he said. 'I won't let you down.'

'I don't care about me,' Sophie said. 'Just don't let Livi down.'

'I won't,' he promised.

He took a black cab from Covent Garden; on the way back to Bayswater, he emailed the photographs to Shelley, and advised her he was going to be working remotely for the rest of the week. He also checked Livi's hotel and booked his train ticket and a hotel—one that wasn't too far from Livi's, but far enough away so she wouldn't feel that he was crowding her—and then texted the details to Sophie, to keep her in the loop.

It didn't take him long to pack a small case, or to get to St Pancras and catch the Eurostar to Brussels.

Hopefully the city was far enough away from London—and, more importantly, from their shared pasts—for Livi to be comfortable sitting down and having a serious talk with him. Did she feel the same way about him as he did about her? He hoped so; all he needed to do now was persuade her that she could trust him.

All, he thought wryly.

CHAPTER NINE

LIVI HAD ALREADY worked out which tram she needed to catch from the station to get to her hotel. When she went up to street level, she discovered that the weather was glorious: blue skies, with just enough of a breeze to stop the air feeling sticky. A perfect summer day. Just what she needed, right now.

It was a while since she'd last travelled to Brussels, and she'd forgotten how pretty the city was, with its gorgeous historic buildings surrounding cobbled squares dotted with fountains, from ancient sculptures to modern steel spheres. Her hotel was in one of the grand old buildings, only a few minutes' walk from the tram stop; she checked in at the reception and made her way up to her room. As soon as she'd made herself a cup of coffee, she sat in the easy chair next to the bed and rang her mum.

'Just to let you know I'm here safely,' she said. 'And I had a really good journey. No delays, and it was easy to find the hotel. I'm just having a coffee while I unpack, then I'm going out to do a bit of exploring.'

'That's great,' Sophie said. 'Um—I need to tell you something, sweetheart. Josh is on his way to Brussels.'

Livi felt her jaw drop. 'Sorry?'

'Josh is on his way,' her mum repeated. 'To see you.'

'How? He doesn't know where I am.'

'I told him,' Sophie said. 'Though he's not going to stay at your hotel.'

'What? But—why is he coming to Brussels? Why did you tell him where I was?' Livi asked, horrified. Her mother had encouraged her to put some distance between them; why had she changed her mind and practically allowed him to hijack her escape to Brussels?

'Livi, I think you both need to talk. And a neutral place would be good for both of you. Better than London. There's nothing to get in the way.'

'So you're taking his side, now?'

'No,' Sophie said. 'But I believe he intends to listen more than he talks. Which is quite rare, in men, in my experience. Including your father.'

'Mum, that's pretty sexist,' Livi said, with a shocked giggle.

'It's also true. Give him a chance, Livi. For both of your sakes.'

When Livi ended the call, she drummed her fingers on the table. So Josh was planning to come and see her? Well, she didn't want to meet him at her hotel. Neutral ground would be better. And he must be at least two hours behind her own departure, she calculated.

At least they wouldn't be staying at the same hotel, so if things went badly it wouldn't be quite so awkward.

She checked out local cafés on the internet, then texted him. Mum tells me you want to talk and you're coming to Brussels. Perhaps you'd like to meet for coffee. There's a nice café not far from my hotel, in the Galeries Hubert. Can check out their waffles at the same time. Assume 4.30 works for you? L.

Keeping it polite and almost businesslike: that was the best way forward, she thought. Meet him in public, and mix it with a bit of work so she could focus on that. Keep all the emotions out of it.

As he arrived at the train station in Brussels, Josh steeled himself not to think of the last time he'd travelled to Brussels, as part of the orchestra. The last six months of his career. He'd played the Bach *chaconne* in the elegant Art Deco hall at the Palais des Beaux-Arts. But that was another world and another life, he reminded himself. He'd made his peace with it, for the most part, but every so often that empty space inside him seemed to gape a little wider—now being one of those times, when the memories seemed to mock him.

He pulled himself together. Just. When he made his way outside the station, a driver was waiting next to a limousine, holding a card saying *Mr Garrett*.

Josh walked over and made himself known, and the chauffeur drove him into the city centre. The hotel was nothing like the one Josh had stayed in, last time he'd been in Brussels; rather than being a modern-built economy-class hotel on the outskirts of the city, this was an ancient red-brick building with stone quoins, in keeping with the historic buildings around it. Wrought-iron balconies sat at the bottom of every tall window, filled with clusters of pots stuffed with bright red geraniums. The marble-floored reception was light and airy, with sparkling chandeliers, and Josh was delighted to discover that his suite was on the top floor. Not only did it have fabulous views over the rooftops of Brussels and plenty of space, the suite also had its own private roof garden, with comfortable chairs set round a table and roses climbing round the willow screens surrounding the terrace, perfuming the air.

Before he unpacked, he unlocked his phone, intending to check in with the office back in London. Then he saw the notification of the text from Livi.

He read it, to discover that Sophie had told her he was on his way, and she'd pre-empted him. Well, OK. At least it seemed she was prepared to talk. That had to be a good thing. He glanced at the time. He had twenty minutes to get to the café. A quick check on his maps app told him it was less than a ten-minute walk from his hotel to the meeting spot.

Then again, would she really open her heart to him in a public place? Maybe here might be a better place to talk. Just the two of them in this lovely roof garden.

4.30 fine, he messaged back. Unless you'd rather come and sit on the roof terrace with me here. Is private and has good views. He took a snap of the terrace, making sure the ornate gothic spire of the town hall with its pinnacles and turrets was in the background, and sent it to her.

Looks nice, but I think neutral ground would be more sensible, she messaged back.

Josh understood where she was coming from; she was clearly trying to set boundaries. It was a valid point. But the kind of conversation they were going to have really needed a more private space than a popular tourist spot.

Agreed, but harder to talk openly in a public space with lots of people around. Bit noisy. Easy to miss things, he messaged.

She rang him. 'Are you trying to call the shots and make me come to you because you have a flashy hotel with a roof garden?'

'No. I'm just thinking it's difficult to have a private conversation in a busy, noisy café stuffed full of people, and here it's quiet,' he said. 'I want to listen to you, Livi, but I also want to say some things I'd be uncomfortable sharing in a public space. Not because I think anyone might recognise me and go running to the press with what they think is gossip—those days are long gone—but because…' He blew out a breath. 'It's just not the kind of thing that's easy to talk about. Especially with people chattering around you.'

'Hmm,' she said. 'Where are you?'

'Just off Grand-Place. Overlooking the town hall.'

'It's less businesslike, meeting at your hotel, but you have a point about privacy,' she said.

'I'll order us something from room service. What would you like? Tea, coffee, a glass of wine?' he asked.

'Tea, please,' she said. 'I'll walk over to you.'

'I'll text you the hotel details and my room number. I'll keep an ear out for you knocking,' he said.

'All right,' she said.

She didn't reply to his text. Then again, he reminded himself, there was no need. He'd given her all the necessary information. What else was there to say?

The waitress had literally just delivered a tray of tea and biscuits and he'd taken it to the table on the terrace when there was a knock on his door. Heart pounding, he opened the door to face Livi.

She looked amazing in jeans, comfortable shoes, a pretty top and a sunhat, and his heart squeezed. He really needed to get this right because, even though he wasn't entirely sure where this was going, he knew he wanted her in his life.

'Well, Mr Garrett. This is a bit flashy. The penthouse suite?' she commented.

'It wasn't *intentionally* flashy. It was the only room they had left, and your mum told me not to book a room at your hotel,' he said.

'I came to Brussels to get some distance and some perspective,' she said. 'I wasn't expecting you to follow me here.'

He could see the tightness in her expression. And he could understand it now: she thought he was intruding on her private space to think. 'I didn't mean to steamroller you or act like a stalker,' he said. 'That honestly wasn't my intention. I just think we need to talk. Face to face. And I thought—hoped—maybe being out of London would make it easier for both of us.'

'Maybe,' she said. 'And this terrace is quiet, you say? You didn't want to meet in a café, but what if other hotel guests want to use the roof terrace?'

'They, um, don't have access to this particular bit,' he said. 'It's part of the suite.'

She blinked. 'You have your *own private roof terrace*?'

'A small one. But yes,' he said, squirming slightly. 'I didn't realise when I booked the room. As I said, this wasn't intentionally flashy. I'm not trying to impress you.' He gave her a wry smile. 'When I saw the terrace I thought it might be a good place to talk, because we're not going to be interrupted by anyone and we'll have some privacy. I'm not trying to take over.'

She didn't look as if she quite believed him, but she let him usher her into the living room area and through the French doors to the roof terrace.

'It's pretty,' she said, walking round the terrace so she could admire all the views, then bending to smell the roses. 'These are proper scented roses, too. And fairy lights.'

Which would make the terrace look incredibly romantic when it was dark. Not that he was going to be stupid enough to say so. Instead, he kept it neutral and asked, 'Can I pour you some tea?'

'Thank you.' There was still that tightness around her eyes as she pulled out the chair opposite the one he was standing behind and sat down. The fact she sat opposite him rather than next to him, with the barrier of a table between them, was telling.

Hopefully she'd relax a bit before they started talking. He knew how to make a client relax, but this wasn't a business discussion. It was a lot more personal than he usually got, and a business technique simply wouldn't work here. He was beginning to think that her tension was affecting him, too. Addling his brain. Because suddenly he felt really out of his depth.

He poured out two cups of tea, leaving her to add her own milk.

'Help yourself,' he said, gesturing to the plate of tiny buttery biscuits.

For a moment, he thought she was going to refuse.

But then she nibbled one and looked critically at it. 'Shortbread thins with salted caramel nuggets. These are seriously good.'

It wasn't the sugar rush that had relaxed her a little bit, he realised; it was seeing things from a business angle.

'I need to up my biscuit game,' she said.

'If your biscuits are the same standard as your raspberry—' Then he stopped dead, remembering what he'd said when he'd tried the *entremet*. About first kisses. And how she'd kissed him. How he'd kissed her back. Everything had gone weirdly skewed after that.

And reminding her of that would be the quickest way to put up another barrier between them. He felt the colour flooding into his face. 'Um, I apologise. That wasn't meant to be…'

'I know.' But she was blushing, too, clearly thinking of exactly the same moments as he was.

He sighed and rested his elbows on the table, linking his fingers into a bridge and resting his chin on it. He looked levelly at her. There was no point in trying to pussyfoot round it anymore. 'We have unfinished business, Livi.'

'We do.' She sighed. 'And it's complicated.'

'I'm listening,' he said.

She raised an eyebrow. 'You're expecting *me* to be the one to sort it out?'

'No,' he said. 'Sorting it out is something we need to do together. But I want to listen to you first, rather than talk over you. Especially as I've already pretty much wrecked your thinking time away—even though that wasn't what I intended.'

She looked serious, clearly digesting what he meant: that he didn't plan to railroad her into doing whatever he wanted. That her views were just as important to him as his own. That he wanted them to work as a team—personally, not just in business. 'I'm not sure where to start,' she said.

'Neither am I,' he said. 'I guess it probably

ought to be *that* night—' the momentous one all those years ago, that had had such a big impact on both their lives '—but that feels…' He shook his head. 'I don't know. Huge. I think that's too much to handle in a single conversation.' Especially with what he wanted to tell her.

'I think it goes back before then, even,' she said. 'I had a crush on you for years and years and years. All the way through my teens. All my mates were drooling over actors and pop stars they'd never get to meet in a million years, and I just wanted you. My big brother's best mate. The epitome of tall, dark and handsome.' She gave him a rueful smile. 'I convinced myself that you were within reach. Except you never were. Because you were just as famous as the actors and pop stars, and just as far away from me as they were from my friends. The fact I knew you in real life didn't make any difference.'

'I saw you as my best friend's little sister. A bit shy, blushed a lot, very sweet, and completely off limits. When I was eighteen, you were still only fourteen,' he reminded her.

A muscle twitched in her jaw. 'A stupid, spotty-faced schoolgirl.'

He flinched, remembering the words he'd

thrown at her. 'It was a horrible thing to say, and it wasn't true.' She hadn't even been a schoolgirl; she'd been twenty, working full time in her family's business. But he'd deliberately said it to make her feel young and small.

'To be fair, I did have terrible skin,' she admitted.

'Lots of people do at that age,' he said. 'And they're often sensitive about it. I was deliberately mean, because I knew it would push you away. I apologise for being so…' He shook his head, unable to think of the right word to describe his behaviour. 'Cruel and horrible, basically. I'm sorry I hurt you.'

She gave a single nod of acknowledgement.

'Plus you've never been stupid, Livi. You're bright. You could've got in to any university you chose, if that was what you'd wanted. But Eti said you wanted to work in the family business.'

'I did. I love what we do at the brasserie,' she said. 'People come to Lambert's for family celebrations, for birthdays and anniversaries and engagements, because they know the food is excellent and there's a good atmosphere. They come to us for first dates, because we have quieter tables where people can talk and get to know each other over good food. They come to us because maybe they've had a bit of a rough week and they're a bit too tired to cook; all they want is to eat some Belgian comfort food or a really fancy dessert, and to have a bit of a fuss made over them. And I love that we're part of people's lives like that, through the good times and the bad. I love that my great-granddad came over from Belgium to London and started it all off; our restaurant's been part of Covent Garden for decades, and I'm part of that tradition. I love that I can produce a dessert that makes people feel special even before I stick a celebratory indoor sparkler in it. It feels as if I'm doing something that actually has meaning.'

'There's no "as if",' he said. 'You *are* doing something that has meaning.' Like he'd once been able to do, with his violin: he'd been able to transport people away from a tricky bit of their lives to a place of joy. What he did nowadays felt as if it was all surface and meaningless. He knew it was important to his clients, because it helped them; but it wasn't the same. It didn't have that personal connection, the way music did.

'Thank you,' she said. 'Anyway. That night happened. And I hated you for a bit, afterwards. But you did at least stay away from me.' She ate another biscuit. 'I dated other guys.' She didn't say it in so many words, but her eyes told him it had been more than just dating. 'It never worked out, but I assumed it was just because I was rubbish at relationships.'

Because what he'd said to her had trashed her confidence and she hadn't let them close in case they hurt her the same way that he had? Guilt pinched him. Hard.

'I really thought I was over you, Josh. When Dad said your agency was the third one pitching, I was a bit shocked, but I honestly thought I'd manage to be all cool and calm—sophisticated was probably a step too far,' she added ruefully, 'but I was managing.' She dragged in a breath. 'Until I kissed you, last night.'

Her eyes went wide, as if she were reliving the kiss, and she suddenly looked lost. He wanted to wrap his arms round her and tell her that everything would be all right, but it wouldn't be. Words just weren't enough to fix this. He didn't know how to fix this, but talking was a start.

'You changed everything for me,' he said. 'Because of you, I went to therapy instead of...' The words stuck in his throat. He couldn't tell her everything just now. It would feel like blackmail. He wanted her to focus on now, not then. Instead, he mumbled, 'I'm sorry I hurt you. I felt horrible when I realised I'd taken your virginity. I didn't have anything to give you back, except the empty shell of who I used to be. I guessed you hoped for more, and I couldn't deliver. That's why I pushed you away.' He shook his head. 'I guess it was a mix of guilt and self-loathing. And I still felt so bad about it, the next morning, that I made the decision to go to therapy and sort my head out. Something I'd been resisting.'

'Why did you resist it?'

'Because I didn't think I was fixable,' he said. 'But my therapist was good. I pretty much came to terms with losing my music and I found something else that I could do. Yes, the empty space inside me is still there, but I can manage it.' Most of the time, but he wasn't going to tell her about the moments when he couldn't. Right now, this wasn't about him and his demons; it was about her. 'And I've never forgiven myself for the way I treated you. That's why I stayed out of your way. I thought if you didn't see me, it would make things easier for you.' He looked at her. 'We didn't really know each other properly, back then. You were my best friend's little sister, and I was focused on my violin. When we started working together on the project, it made me realise things weren't the same. You still have that kindness, that sweetness I remember—but I'm seeing a different side of you, now. The grown-up, professional you. Your cooking blows me away.'

She went pink. 'Thank you.'

'It's not a compliment. It's a statement of fact,' he said. 'This isn't like when I first met you, when I was a snotty-nosed kid and you weren't much more than a toddler. Or when you were a shy teenager and I was focused on my music to the exclusion of everything and everyone else. Or when my life imploded and…' He stopped, still unable to voice what he'd nearly done. If he ever told her about that, he'd need to choose his words very carefully. 'When I was incredibly unfair to you,' he said instead, his voice thick with emotion. 'Now, the four years between us don't matter anymore. And I like the woman you've become, Livi. I really, *really* like you. I want to reset our relationship. And I'm not talking about our business relationship—I mean you and me. I want to start again, get to know each other properly outside work.'

She swallowed hard. 'I don't know if I can do that, Josh.'

'Maybe we can start as friends,' he said. 'Though I'd like it to become more than that.'

'It's all...a bit overwhelming,' she said. 'That's why I came here a couple of days early for my course. To put some space between us and think about how to deal with things between you and me.'

'And I've trashed that by following you here. I don't mean to crowd you,' he said. 'But I do need you to know I'm sincere. I'm so sorry about the way I treated you, back then. I'd like to think that if I hadn't been in such a bad place, I would've been kinder to you. Even so, I know I've changed over the last eight years. Will you let me prove myself to you? Here, where we don't have any memories to get in the way. Where it's just you and me. Obviously you're here to do your course, and I'm not going to interfere with that—I can work remotely when you're busy. But when you're not in class, I'd like to spend some time with you. Take you to dinner somewhere the food's really good, talk with you, maybe hold your hand.' He gave her a wry smile. 'And I promise I won't kiss you again until you ask me to.'

'Time together. Just getting to know each other again,' she said.

He nodded. 'Will you give me a second chance?'

CHAPTER TEN

A SECOND CHANCE. Get to know each other again. Reset their relationship.

It was oh, so tempting. And he made it sound oh, so easy.

But Livi had cried an ocean over Josh, eight years ago. She didn't want to repeat her mistake and end up with that kind of misery filling her heart again. How could she be sure a relationship would work between them, this time round?

And was that what she wanted? Was Josh who she wanted?

Josh had apologised for what had happened. Sincerely. She understood why he'd lashed out at her, back then, and she could even forgive it.

The problem was, she couldn't forget it. And part of her wondered if it would happen again. Life didn't tend to run smoothly. The next time things became tricky for Josh, would he push her away again rather than talk it through with her? Would he see her as his equal, now, or would he be stubborn and feel he had to protect her out of some misplaced sense of chivalry?

She took a sip of tea and thought about it.

Brussels wasn't London. Here, there were no memories. At least, not for her; she suspected that Josh had probably played the violin in a concert hall somewhere here, along with stages in many other European cities. But, together, they could make this a fresh start for both of them.

And she noticed that he was being patient. Sipping tea, relaxing on the terrace, not pressuring her to make a decision or to talk until she was ready. He meant it about giving her space.

OK.

If he could do this, so could she.

'We could,' she said carefully, 'give it a try. See how it goes.'

'Thank you,' he said. 'I'd really like that.' He paused. 'Perhaps we can go for a walk, when we've finished the tea. Take in some of the sights of the city, see if we can spot any of the Tintin cartoons on the walls of buildings.'

'OK,' she said. 'Actually, I spent most of

the journey from St Pancras looking up places to go.'

'Did you make a list of things you wanted to do?' he asked.

She nodded. 'There are some cafés and chocolate shops I really want to visit, partly to see what's on offer for afternoon tea and if there are any ideas that I could tweak a bit to suit me. And the art galleries.'

'Sounds good,' he said. 'And if the weather's nice maybe we can go for a walk through one of the parks.'

'That sounds good, too,' she said.

'And maybe we can have dinner tonight? We could find a place that takes our fancy, while we're out; or if you'd like to see what this roof terrace looks like after dark, the hotel has a menu that looks pretty good.'

'Just so you know, I judge menus by the desserts,' she said.

He took out his phone, went into the hotel's website and found the dessert menu, then handed his phone to her. 'Does it pass your test?'

She looked through it and smiled. 'Waffles. Well, I think any place should offer them for dessert in Brussels,' she said. 'And *merveilleux*.'

'Wonderful?' he translated.

She chuckled. 'Meringue. With cherries and white chocolate, in this case. Hmm. Ice cream and sorbets, served with *speculoos* biscuits. Or *pain perdu*—French toast, with salted caramel and apples. And obviously a *dame blanche*—vanilla ice cream sundae with warm chocolate sauce.' She spotted the last item on the menu. 'Oh, now this has my name on it. Almond semifreddo with blueberry compote. Thank you, dinner here will be lovely. With the fairy lights.'

He grinned. 'I love your enthusiasm. And I'll make a special request for them to save you a piece of the semifreddo in case they run out.'

'I appreciate that,' she said. 'That's kind.'

'I want you to enjoy dinner—which is my treat, by the way.'

'Only if you let me buy you dinner tomorrow,' she warned. 'Because if we're going to have any kind of relationship—whether it's business, friendship or something more—we're going to do it as equals.'

'I accept with pleasure,' he said, smiling.

And just like that it was easy.

Josh had a quiet word at the reception desk before they went exploring; he booked dinner and made sure that Livi's chosen dessert would be available, and then they wandered through the narrow street into the cobbled square of Grand-Place. The architecture was really stunning; the buildings all had fancy gables and lead roofs. Some had gold details over windows and on pillars; one had a gold statue of a man on a horse on the roof, while another had a gold plaque of a peacock, and others had statues in niches.

'According to this,' she said, reading from the guidebook on her phone, 'most of the buildings were for different guilds, and each house has its own name.' She pointed out one of the houses. 'That one, *Le Pigeon*, was for the city's painters, and it's where Victor Hugo lived when he was first exiled from France. And Marx and Engels wrote their manifesto over there in *Le Cygne*.' A sculpture of a swan, framed by greenery and his wings highlighted with gilding, stood above the doorway. 'The guilds were abolished at the end of the eighteenth century, but if my hunch is right and my forebears all followed the same trade as my great-grandfather, working in a kitchen in an inn, then they would probably have been associated with either the brewers' guild or the bakers' guild.' She pointed out a building with gilded hop plants twining round its columns.

'*L'Arbre D'Or* was the brewers; and the one over there with the dome, *Le Roy d'Espagne*, was the bakers.'

'*Le Roy d'Espagne.* The King of Spain,' he translated.

'It says here the building was named after Charles II, who was the King of Spain when it was built in 1697, and he was also the king of the southern Netherlands—which included Belgium,' she said. 'All the statues on the balustrade are about baking—Hercules having the strength you need to be a baker, Ceres obviously as the goddess of agriculture being linked to wheat, Mercury for the fire in the oven, Neptune for the water in the dough, Minerva with her hourglass for timing the length of the bake, and a woman with a windmill—not a goddess, but she probably should be. Oh, and Saint-Aubert, the patron saint of bakers, is above the door.'

They spent a while with her guidebook, enjoying picking out which house had belonged to which guild.

'Do you know where your great-grandfather lived or worked?' he asked.

'As it happens, I do. Jean Lambert was born in 1907, and he worked in an auberge called *Le Cheval Rouge* in the old part of town, not that far from here—a street off a street off Grand-Place,' she said. 'The family didn't actually own the auberge, but they ran it. It changed hands a few times, and then it became a chocolate shop for a while and then a boutique selling handbags, but now it's a bar again and they've resurrected the old name, which is lovely.' She smiled. 'I've got the address; I was going to check it out and take some photos of what it looks like now for Dad, and maybe have a chat with whoever runs it now and show them the photos we have of my great-granddad when he worked here. With any luck, they might even have photos of the inn from further back that they can share with me.'

'You've got the photos with you?' Josh asked.

'They're on my phone,' she said, and picked out an album from her photos app to show him. 'That's Jean Lambert, in the bar at *Le Cheval Rouge*, in the late 1920s. It's a bit blurry, but he's the one with the beard wearing a white apron and a chef's cap.'

'What made him move to London?' Josh asked.

'My great-grandmother, Elsie,' she said. 'Her dad was in the rag trade. When he came on a business trip to Brussels, Elsie accompanied him. Her dad bought lace from several people, including from Jean Lambert's mum, Marie-Thérèse. Marie-Thérèse told them *Le Cheval Rouge* was a good place to have dinner, and said to mention her name at the bar as her son would give them a discount. Family legend is that it was love at first sight between Jean and Elsie. When Elsie's dad had finished his business dealings and they went back to London, Jean followed them to London and persuaded her dad to let her marry him.'

'And that's their wedding photo?' he asked, turning to the next shot.

'In April 1934,' she said. 'Christ Church, in Spitalfields.'

'Look at all that lace,' he said. 'Her dress and her veil.'

She nodded. 'Isn't it gorgeous? The lace was made by Jean's mum, and Elsie's dad made the wedding dress. My grandparents donated it to the V&A museum so other people could enjoy it, too—it's a part of East End history.'

'So you could've ended up being a dress designer instead of a *pâtissière*,' he said.

'In theory, perhaps, but in practice I'm hopeless at crafts apart from sugar-craft,' she said with a smile. 'It was the cooking side that seemed to stick in the family. Elsie's family lived in Spitalfields, and there were a lot of Huguenots working in the rag trade there. Jean set up a stall selling Belgian comfort food—*stoemp*, sausages, *moules-frites* and carbonnade Flamande.'

'All things that are still on your menu today,' he said.

She was glad he got it. 'Yes. The stall was really popular, and did well enough that when a local café came up for sale Jean could afford to buy it and expand the business. Things were a bit tricky during the war—luckily as a Belgian, Jean wasn't treated as an enemy alien and stuck in an internment camp, but he went off to fight with the English troops. The clothing factory took a direct hit, so Elsie took over the café and ran it until Jean came home.' She gave a rueful smile. 'Sadly, Elsie and Jean both died before I was born, so I never got to know them. But I do remember my granddad. He joined his mum and dad in running the café in Spitalfields, and he moved it to Covent Garden back in the 1960s, just before my dad was born. Back then, his customers were mainly the market workers, so he opened early to get the breakfast trade, and finished when they finished. When the fruit and veg market moved to Nine Elms in the 1970s, Dad was in charge and he turned Lambert's into the brasserie it is now, serving dinner rather than breakfast. And now it's my turn to mix things up a bit.'

'This would all be a great social media story,' Josh said. 'We definitely need to do a page on your website showing how everything changed over the years and what's remained constant. Four generations of Lamberts cooking for their customers and changing to meet their needs. We can drip-feed the story, telling a little bit more each week and including a new photo, so people come back for the next instalment.'

'Dad's got a lot more photos. I'm sure he'd be happy to go through them with you,' Livi said.

'And a link to your own speciality would be good. Maybe we could run a story on the wedding cakes?' he suggested. 'I know you don't make wedding cakes—'

'Actually, I made Eti and Lucy's,' she corrected. 'But you're right in that I don't make occasion cakes as a rule.'

He looked thoughtful. 'I wonder if all the wedding cakes in your family over the years were made by someone in the family? If so, there might even be a link back to the lace, with maybe the patterns on the wedding cake being inspired by the patterns of the lace in the bride's veil.'

'I never even thought of that,' Livi said. 'I wish I had. Lucy had a lace veil. I could've made the cake decorations in matching sugar paste and it would've looked amazing.'

'Eti and Lucy's cake looked amazing in the photographs,' Josh said, and she remembered that he'd deliberately given her space so she wouldn't feel awkward at the wedding. 'He sent me a bit, too. Best wedding cake I've ever tasted, and I'm not just saying that.'

She dipped her head to acknowledge the compliment. 'I'm pretty sure my granddad made Mum and Dad's wedding cake, so Dad can tell us about that,' she said. 'I'm not sure about the generations before, but Dad might know. I'm guessing at the very least he has the wedding photos somewhere, so we can enlarge the cakes and the veil to take a closer look.'

Josh made a note. 'This is going to be fun,' he said. 'Shall we go and find the auberge?'

Livi had already been looking forward to doing the little bit of family history research, but Josh's enthusiasm made her enjoy it even more. They made their way down one of the side streets from Grand-Place, noting the cobbles on the streets and the old-fashioned streetlamps, then turned down another street, and from there took another turning.

'Here it is,' she said. 'Dad's going to love the bar's sign.' It was a very modern stylised horse's head, entirely in red, with a flying mane.

'Let me take a picture of you under it,' Josh suggested. 'My phone or yours?'

'Mine, please—then I can send the photos to Dad, later,' she said.

She posed for the photograph, then Josh took a shot of the bar's sign before they went in and ordered two beers. Luckily the owner was actually working behind the bar, and when Livi told him about their quest he joined them at their table and was thrilled to see the photographs of her great-grandfather working at the old auberge. 'What a fantastic link to the past. Would you be kind enough to send me a copy so I can print them out and put them in a frame on the wall with the ones I already have?' he asked. 'My customers would love to see them.'

He showed them the history wall, with pictures of the auberge from the middle of the last century, the shops that had taken its place, and even woodcuts of the inn as it had been a century before Jean Lambert and his family had run it. 'I've got copies of all of these on my laptop. I'll send them to you,' he promised, and they exchanged business cards along with a promise that he'd come and have dinner with them, next time he was in London.

'That was a good result,' Josh said as they headed back to his hotel.

'Agreed,' she said.

And then she tripped on the cobbles.

'Whoa,' Josh said, catching her arm so she didn't fall flat on her face. 'Are you OK, Livi?'

'I'm fine. Thanks for rescuing me,' she said.

'No problem,' he said with a smile that made her feel all gooey inside.

She was disappointed when he let her arm go, missing the warmth of his skin against hers.

But as they walked on, their hands brushed against each other. She wasn't sure whose fingers clung to whose, but suddenly they were holding hands. Properly. As if they were dating for real.

Her heart rate went up a notch. Was this what it would be like, dating Josh? As a teenager, she'd dreamed of walking along a beach with him, holding hands. Teenage Livi would've been beside herself to think this was actually happening.

She stole a glance at him. He looked utterly insouciant—or did he? Was there a slight wariness in his face, as if he too couldn't quite believe they were walking together, holding hands?

Well, OK. She wasn't going to break the bubble by commenting on it. And they were supposed to be seeing how things went. 'I was thinking, there are a few lace shops in the city that have historic collections. Maybe we can drop in to a couple tomorrow and see if they have any information about Jean's mum, or know where we might be able to find out?'

'That's a good idea,' he said.

When they reached the hotel, he stopped holding her hand so he could open the door for her. She smiled her thanks, then let him usher her into the lift and up to his penthouse apartment.

It was still too early for the fairy lights to have come on, but she enjoyed the late evening sun on the roof terrace. Particularly after they'd ordered dinner and a bottle of wine: white asparagus with truffle vinaigrette, ravioli with burrata, and scallops with a saffron beurre blanc served with sweet potato puree and tenderstem broccoli. Josh ordered cheese where she'd opted for the almond semifreddo with blueberry sauce.

'Would you like an aperitif?' he asked.

'Europe and summer always says Aperol spritz to me,' she said.

'Perfect. I'll join you,' he said.

While they were waiting for their drinks to arrive, Livi sent her father the photographs of *Le Cheval Rouge* and asked him for the photographs she and Josh had discussed earlier.

'This feels like a proper holiday,' she said when their spritzes arrived on a silver salver, in gorgeous glassware and garnished with a twist of blood orange. 'Sitting on a terrace in the sun, sipping a cocktail.'

'Is that your normal kind of holiday?' he asked. 'Or do you like relaxing on a beach?'

'Beach holidays aren't my kind of thing. I'd get twitchy after a day of sitting doing nothing,' she said. 'I prefer city breaks, where I can explore somewhere. Art galleries, culture and food, that's what I like best.' She looked at him. 'What about you?'

He winced. 'I've never been very good at holidays. In my younger days, obviously I travelled a lot for work and didn't get to see very much of the places I visited; and then I kind of didn't really want to go back and see what I'd missed.'

'So what do you do for holidays now?' she asked.

'I don't really take them,' he said. 'Maybe a few odd days here and there. I might go to an exhibition at a museum. I like Bath.'

'For Austen?' she asked.

'Herschel,' he said, surprising her. 'And the curse tablets at the Roman baths.' He smiled and took a sip of his spritz. 'This is much, much nicer than lukewarm sulphurous spring water.'

'The Austen side of things is fun,' she said. 'Dressing up to go to a proper Regency ball, especially when the dance floor's been chalked with some gorgeous pattern.'

'You like dancing?' he asked.

'I do,' she said. 'But I'm guessing that's something you'd rather avoid.'

'Yeah,' he admitted. He lifted one shoulder in a half-shrug. 'My parents have nagged me into joining them when they've hired a little cottage on the North Norfolk coast. I like taking the dog for a walk on the beach to watch the sun rise and set, or staying out late in the middle of summer to watch for meteors.'

'You're not tempted to get a dog yourself?' she asked.

'I've thought about it,' he admitted. 'A big soppy golden retriever who'd be the office mascot, sitting under my desk and taking a nap with his head on my feet, then getting his share of the sofa back at the house.'

He sounded a bit wistful. Was he lonely? Livi wondered. Because, apart from his team at work, he seemed to keep at a distance from people. Eti was probably the closest one to him, but her brother had mentioned that it was hard to pin Josh down. Because he'd been trying to avoid her? Or did seeing Eti remind him too much of what he'd lost? Not that she could ask without being pushy, and she didn't want him to back away.

'How about you?' he asked.

Of course he wasn't asking if she was lonely. She was probably reading too much into it. He probably wanted to know if she wanted a dog. 'It wouldn't be fair to keep a dog, working restaurant hours,' she said. And her hours weren't really going to change, were they?

Just as it was starting to feel a tiny bit awkward, there was a knock at the door and their first course arrived.

'It's beautifully plated,' Livi said, looking

critically at the white asparagus with truffle vinaigrette. 'It looks like a work of art.'

'And it tastes even better,' Josh said, after his first mouthful.

'Is everything OK in the office?' she asked.

'It's fine. I know if there's a problem my team will get in touch,' he said. 'And it does them good to know I trust them to get on with things rather than micromanaging.' He looked wistful. 'I quite envy you the fact you're the fourth generation in the family business. All that history.'

'Would you have wanted to follow your father into stockbroking or your mum into teaching?' she asked.

'No,' he admitted. 'I knew what I wanted to do really early on, even though nobody in the family had ever gone past grade five piano. I just loved the feeling music gave me—as if I was fully alive, right in the moment, whether it was learning to shriek my way through *Three Blind Mice* on the recorder at infant school, or doing endless scales and arpeggios on the piano. The first piece I learned on the piano was Bach's *Minuet in G*—though actually it was written by Christian Petzold, and it was attributed to JS Bach because Anna Magdalena, his wife, copied it into her notebook. I liked the *Minuet in G minor* more, though. That always felt like sunshine falling across a garden on a late winter afternoon.'

'I don't know the pieces,' she said.

'You would if you heard them,' he said. 'Definitely the G major.'

She almost asked him to hum them for her, but maybe that would be pushing him too far.

'I'll send you a link, later,' he said.

He clearly missed music, Livi thought, noting that he hadn't mentioned the moment he'd first picked up a violin; clearly that was too much for him to bear remembering. Though she was sure if he allowed himself to listen to music, he'd get the joy back that he'd first experienced as a small child. Not as much as if he could still play, admittedly, but surely it would be better for him than denying himself that pleasure for the rest of his life?

The waitress came to collect their plates and deliver the next course—ravioli with the creamiest, wobbliest burrata, followed by tender scallops in the most delicious saffron beurre blanc, nestled on a bed of sweet potato puree and tenderstem purple broccoli.

Livi kept the conversation light for the rest of the meal.

The semifreddo was as wonderful as she'd

hoped, and so were the salted caramel pralines that came with the exceptionally good coffee.

'Thank you for dinner,' she said when she'd finished the last sip of coffee.

'My pleasure,' he said. 'It was good to spend time with you today.'

'I really enjoyed it, too,' she admitted. 'I'll see you tomorrow, then.'

'I'll walk you back to your hotel,' he said.

'It's only a few minutes away,' she said. 'I think I can manage.'

'You're an adult, and you can look after yourself,' he said. 'I know. But humour me?'

'All right,' she said.

He took her hand again as they walked through Grand-Place again. What could be more romantic, she thought, than wandering through ancient cobbled streets, hand in hand? It was a moment to savour and enjoy.

Josh saw her safely to the door of her hotel. 'See you tomorrow,' he said. 'Shall I call for you?'

'Lovely. About ten?' she suggested. 'Then maybe we can go looking for the lacemakers.'

'It's a date,' he said softly.

And, even though he didn't actually kiss her goodnight—he'd said earlier that he wouldn't kiss her again until she asked him to—the warmth in his eyes felt like a hug.

'It's a date,' she agreed.

In some ways, it'd be their first real date. Their first *official* date, at least. And it was weird how the idea made her blood feel fizzy.

A few minutes later, he texted her the links to the piano pieces he'd talked about. She recognised the first one immediately, but not the second. Like sunshine on a winter afternoon, he'd said: and she could hear what he meant.

Ten points to you, she texted back. You're right, I did recognise the first one. I didn't know the second, but I prefer it. I see what you mean about winter sunshine.

Sweet dreams, he texted back. Try this one to fall asleep to. It's the musical equivalent of Monet's garden.

He'd sent her a link to Debussy's *Rêverie*, another piece she didn't really know but liked instantly.

If sharing music with her would help to give him his music back, then maybe dating him properly would help her to get her trust in relationships back, she thought.

Maybe they could fix each other.

Maybe.

CHAPTER ELEVEN

JOSH WOKE ON Wednesday morning feeling happier than he could remember feeling in years. Which was ridiculous. Just because Livi had agreed to spend the day with him, he really shouldn't get carried away.

Even so, he almost started singing in the shower—something he hadn't been minded to do for a very long time. Not since before the accident.

And he couldn't wait to see her.

He caught up with his work while he ate breakfast; then the alarm on his phone pinged to let him know that it was time to go and meet Livi. He texted her to let her know that he was on his way, and she texted straight back. See you in the foyer.

He walked into the hotel reception and saw her straightaway. Today she was wearing a pretty summer dress, teamed with comfortable canvas shoes; she was carrying her floppy sunhat and her sunglasses were perched on the top of her head. He raised his hand in acknowledgement, and she stood up.

'Hi,' he said. And then he felt like a prize fool. 'This is kind of ridiculous, but I'm not sure how to greet you today,' he said. 'Shaking your hand would be too formal, but I can't…' He might as well be honest. 'It doesn't feel right to give you a hug and kiss your cheek yet, either. Not when we agreed to take it slowly.'

'It's been a while since I last dated and I've forgotten the etiquette, too,' she admitted ruefully. 'Shall we just pretend we've greeted each other, for now?'

'Good idea,' he said. Better than feeling awkward. 'You look lovely, by the way.'

'Thank you.' She smiled at him, and his heart skipped a beat. 'You look nice, too.'

He'd thought ridiculously hard about what to wear, not wanting to be too casual but not wanting to look stuffy, either; in the end he'd picked dark tailored trousers and a white collarless linen shirt teamed with black suede lace-up shoes, and added sunglasses and an olive-green bucket hat as a nod to the sunshine.

'Thank you,' he said. 'So we're starting at the Galeries Hubert?'

'We are,' she confirmed. 'And then we're

going in search of antique Belgian lace and Marie-Thérèse Lambert.'

The Galeries Hubert turned out to be a beautiful arcade with a covered glass roof.

'I checked the guidebook this morning,' she said. 'It was built nearly two hundred years ago, and apparently it was once known as the Umbrella of Brussels, because you could go to all the different shops without getting wet when it was raining.'

It was a gorgeously light and airy space, Josh thought, filled with a mixture of shops and cafés and high-end jewellers. The large square windows of the shops and cafés were topped by graceful arched fanlight windows, separated by marble pilasters; the upper floors had niches displaying statues and gorgeous plasterwork. The cafés all had small bistro tables and chairs outside, and patrons were enjoying coffee and delicate pastries.

'This is lovely,' he said. 'I assume there are lace shops in the Galeries?'

'There are,' she said.

As they walked along the Galeries, window-shopping, their hands brushed against each other. Even though they'd held hands yesterday, Josh reminded himself that Livi needed to make the first move, not him. To his delight, the next time their hands brushed, her fingers caught his.

Exactly what he'd hoped would happen.

Without comment, he let her link her fingers properly with his. And how lovely it was to just walk with her through the arcades, holding hands: another cautious step closer to each other.

They went into one of the lace shops, and spent a while browsing some of the antique pieces on display, before chatting to one of the assistants about Livi's great-great-grandmother Marie-Thérèse and the lace she'd made.

'There was a lace centre at Brugge as well as at Bruxelles,' the assistant said. 'The *béguinages*—not quite convents, because the religious women who lived in the community didn't take nun's vows—ran lace schools to teach the local girls a trade. The girls would sit in rows with a stand holding a pillow in front of them, which had pins pricking the pattern out. They'd wind the flax round wooden bobbins, and they'd use the bobbins to weave the lace. Belgian flax gives the finest strands in the world, and makes the most delicate lace.' She smiled. 'I can show you pictures of the girls back at the same kind of time that Marie-Thérèse was working, and I can show you a video of someone making lace in the city more recently.'

'I'd love to see that, please, if you have the time,' Livi said.

Josh, too, was fascinated by the way the lace was woven, the wooden bobbins clattering and then the lacemaker stopping to move a pin before swiftly moving the bobbins again. 'How do they know which bobbin to move where?' he asked.

'Practice,' the assistant said with a smile. 'They actually only work with two pairs of bobbins at a time. They're either making a cross movement, when the left bobbin moves over the right—or a twist movement, when the right bobbin moves over the left. But in a complex pattern, you just see the lace-worker's fingers flying between what looks like a hundred bobbins, and the lace gradually taking shape.'

'There's no way I'd ever be able to do that,' Livi said, sounding awestruck. 'I can do sugarcraft, but I can't even crochet. I could see Holly taking this up, though.'

Josh bought a delicate lace square for his mother, and Livi bought a similar one. 'I'm going to have this framed with a photograph of Marie-Thérèse, and put it up in the brasserie,' she said. 'I'd like to do a history wall like the one in *Le Cheval Rouge*.'

When they'd finished wandering through the galleries—again holding hands as they walked, to Josh's pleasure—they stopped at one of the little cafés for coffee and *speculoos* biscuits that had been stamped with the maker's logo.

'I think your idea of a Lambert's stamp for the biscuits is a good one,' Livi said to Josh. 'Something simple. Maybe just the name embossed across the top, with a rose from an old-fashioned lace design underneath?'

'I can ask Indira, our designer, to mock up some ideas for you,' Josh said. 'If you can find some examples online as a kind of mood board for the brief, send them over to me and I'll get it sorted.'

'All right,' she said with a smile.

They spent the rest of the morning in the old part of the city, window-shopping. In the afternoon, they headed up to the royal quarter; the palace was closed so they couldn't visit the state rooms, but they enjoyed strolling through the formal gardens at the front of the palace and the beautiful park.

Once they'd had their fill in the art galleries, they walked back to Grand-Place via the garden on the Mont des Arts with its beautiful flower beds, clipped topiary, roses and fountains and amazing view of the city. They found a restaurant in a beautiful Art Deco building, with stunning floral stained-glass windows, and the food was presented exquisitely: a starter of a Belgian specialty of smoked salmon croquettes, followed by grilled sea bass with fresh herb mousseline and exquisitely cooked vegetables, and finally a vacherin.

'This is the sort of dessert you make, isn't it?' Josh asked.

Livi nodded. 'The vacherin goes back a couple of centuries; originally, it was a cake, and then a French pastry chef invented the meringue version, layering fruit and ice cream and whipped cream with meringue. It's crisper than a pavlova, though.' She tasted a mouthful. 'Oh, I like their take on it. They've soaked the strawberries in limoncello, and flavoured the whipped cream with it as well. And that's seriously good vanilla ice cream in the layers.'

'The top looks really pretty,' Josh said. 'Are those crystallised violets?'

'And tiny wild strawberries,' she confirmed.

'I like that meringue swan.'

She looked thoughtful. 'We could have a

lace swan instead of a lace rose on the *speculoos* biscuits. I'll take a look at the lace patterns and see what would work best.'

'What would you like to do tomorrow?' he asked.

'I'd quite like to go to Bruges for the day, especially after the assistant said it was an important lacemaking centre,' she admitted. 'Holly went there, a couple of years ago, and she says it's so pretty with all the canals. The Venice of the North.'

He checked his phone. 'It's two hours from here by car, or an hour by train.'

'Much quicker by train. The train's greener, too,' she said.

'If we go early, to make the most of our time, I could ask my hotel to make us a picnic breakfast for the journey,' he suggested.

'That'd be lovely,' she said.

After dinner, he walked her back to her hotel. 'Good night, Livi. I'll text you to confirm the train times and tickets,' he promised.

'Good night, Josh. And thank you for a lovely day,' she said.

He looked at her. 'I didn't know how to greet you, this morning,' he said. 'And I don't know how to say good night.' He badly wanted to kiss her, but he absolutely wouldn't do that unless she asked. He'd made a promise and he intended to stick to it.

'This, I think, is appropriate,' she said, and stood on tiptoe to kiss him on the cheek.

Every nerve-end tingled where her lips had brushed against his skin.

'May I?' he asked, hoping she hadn't noticed how croaky his voice sounded. 'Kiss your cheek, I mean?'

She nodded, blushing, and he did so.

Crazy.

This felt more as if they were teenagers rather than being twenty-eight and thirty-two, respectively. But, at the same time, taking things this slowly took all the pressure off and left just the sweetness—and in a world where everything was so fast-paced and urgent, that was refreshing.

'Sweet dreams,' he said.

And he smiled all the way back to the hotel.

On Thursday morning, Livi headed for the tram stop where she was meeting Josh to go to the train station, and they arrived at almost the same time. The journey to Bruges was comfortable—he'd bought first-class seats, giving them more room, and his hotel had made them a wonderful breakfast of pastries, fruit and freshly squeezed orange juice. Better still, all the packaging was recyclable.

They spent the morning strolling through the narrow streets, enjoying the architecture; the gothic city hall was stunning, with its tall arched windows, turrets and spires. There were lots of colourfully painted buildings with Flemish stepped gables, and Livi couldn't resist taking several snaps of their reflections in the canals. The market square was dominated by its enormous thirteenth-century belfry tower; they climbed the 366 steps to the top for an amazing view over the city, and also spotted the wooden keyboard and foot pedals used to ring the carillon in the belfry floor above.

Livi's 'must see' guidebook directed them to Minnewater Park. 'It's named after the water nymphs—the *minnen*, in Dutch—that were believed to live there in medieval times,' she said. 'Though it's also known as the Lake of Love. So the story goes, a girl called Minna fell in love with a warrior called Stromberg, but her father wanted her to marry a rich nobleman. She ran away and was found perished on the shores of the lake. Stromberg buried her beneath the lake and said their love would last for ever.'

'That's a very sad story,' Josh said, 'for such a pretty park.'

And it really was gorgeous; the bridge across the lake, the lock-house with its stepped gables and ornate turrets, the willow trees and the swans swimming majestically across the water.

'On a more prosaic note,' she said, 'it was also once the docks for Bruges; merchants would bring in spices, silk, wool and wine, and leave with Flemish cloth and lace. Speaking of lace, the Béguinage is near here.'

'Where the nuns taught local girls to make lace,' he said, clearly remembering what the assistant in the lace shop had told them, the previous day.

To Livi's pleasure, the complex—with its beautiful white buildings and courtyard gardens—was open and they were able to look round. One of the assistants also directed them to the lace museum, based in the renovated building of the lacemaking school, and she was fascinated to see a live demonstration of lacemaking. The lacemaker had been plying her craft for more than sixty years, and when Livi showed her the picture of Marie-Thérèse and explained that her great-great-grandmother had been a lacemaker, she guided Livi through how to manipulate the bobbins and then move the pins to their next position.

'I have even more respect now for my great-great-grandma,' Livi said after a couple of minutes. 'Because it would take me at least ten times as long as it takes you to make the lace, and I think mine would come out with holes in the wrong places.'

The elderly lacemaker smiled. 'It comes with practice, my dear. But I'm glad it's given you an idea of what she did for a living.'

They stopped for lunch in a pretty little bistro off one of the little squares. 'These have to be the best *frites* I've ever eaten,' Livi said with a contented sigh.

In the afternoon, they wandered through art galleries and took a boat trip along the canal, and Livi was thrilled to photograph a bevy of swans gliding together under a bridge near the Béguinage, as well as more of the gorgeous architecture. Best of all, Josh sat with his arm round her through the whole trip, making her feel cherished.

Their second official date.

Maybe tonight they might kiss—she remembered he'd told her that he wouldn't kiss her again unless she asked. Maybe tonight she'd ask him; and this time she wouldn't panic.

'Your course is tomorrow,' Josh said eventually. 'It wouldn't be fair to make you stay up late when you're going to be busy. Let's go back now, and have dinner on my roof terrace. We can chill out in the last of the sunshine with a glass of wine.'

'That sounds wonderful,' she said.

They bought coffee to keep them going on the return train journey, then walked slowly back to his hotel off Grand-Place. The menu had changed again that evening; Livi chose violet artichokes, served with a lemon dressing and burrata and garnished with capers and a twist of frisée, followed by chicken with tarragon sauce on a bed of potato puree with snow peas and baby carrots, and finally a tarte tatin flambéed with Calvados and served with ice cream flecked with vanilla seeds.

'That was wonderful,' Livi said when she'd eaten the praline that came with the coffee. She gave a sigh of contentment. 'I'd better head back, because I want to re-read a few things before tomorrow.'

'I'll walk you back,' Josh said.

When they reached the street outside her hotel, he asked, 'Obviously you have your course tomorrow, but what are your plans for the evening?'

'I'd originally thought to have dinner with the others on the course,' she said. 'But that was before I knew you were going to be here.'

'Don't change your plans for me. Mixing with the other course delegates is half the fun,' he said with a smile. 'But maybe we can meet afterwards for a cocktail or something, if you're free?'

'That'd be lovely. I'll text you when we're done and let you know where we are,' she said.

'OK. I'm going to have a day thinking about a new project,' he said, 'so I'll find a nice park to walk through while I'm thinking, and then I'm going to catch up with paperwork—and brief Indira, if you have time to send me the kind of lace patterns you want.'

'I'll take a look before I do my reading,' she promised. 'See you tomorrow night.'

'Enjoy your class,' he said. 'See you tomorrow.'

Was he really going to leave without kissing her goodnight? 'This is our second date. I think a kiss goodnight is just about allowable,' she said lightly.

'A kiss goodnight,' he repeated, his voice satisfyingly husky.

And it would be relatively chaste, given that they were in public. *Safe.*

He closed the gap between them, and stroked her cheek with the backs of his fingers. She tilted her head towards him, and he bent to brush his lips against hers—the softest, sweetest kiss.

The last time he'd kissed her, fireworks had gone off in her head.

This time, it felt like walking through an orchard on soft clouds of apple blossom: warm and sweet and promising.

'Good night,' he said softly when he broke the kiss. 'Sweet dreams.'

And she rather thought they would be.

CHAPTER TWELVE

ALTHOUGH JOSH HAD planned to find a little park to walk through in the morning while he thought about his new project, he spent his time catching up with work on his quiet roof terrace instead, finding the little garden just as inspiring as a park; he ordered lunch and dinner through room service, and he'd just shut down his laptop and was about to chill out with a book when his phone pinged with a text from Livi. Finished dinner. Meet you outside your hotel in fifteen minutes?

Which gave him enough time for a quick shower and change. See you then, he messaged back.

Just as he walked through the front door of the hotel, he saw Livi walking towards him, and raised a hand in acknowledgement.

'How was your course?' he asked.

'Fabulous. We spent the morning working on tempering chocolate.'

'Which is?'

'Melting, cooling and reheating the chocolate so it has a stable structure,' she said. 'If you do it properly, the chocolate will have the right kind of "snap" when it's broken, it'll be smooth rather than grainy, and you'll get that lovely glossy finish. If you don't,' she added, 'the chocolate will go crumbly, it'll look dull or streaky or have a white bloom on it, it might crack when you take it out of the mould, and the mouthfeel won't be good. And you need different kinds of chocolate for moulds and enrobing.'

'Got it,' he said.

'We made pralines in the afternoon,' she said. 'Which was noisy and fun.'

'Noisy?' he asked.

She grinned. 'Once you've tempered your chocolate, you fill the moulds, scrape the chocolate off the top, then rattle the mould against the worktop to get rid of air bubbles—we sounded like a class of tap-dancers! There's a bit more rattling later, after you've filled the praline.'

'And did you eat them all in class, or did you take some home?' he asked.

'Both,' she said.

He coughed. 'That *was* a hint.'

'What, you were expecting a sample of my work?' She chuckled. 'Well, now. That depends. Have you been a good boy, Mr Garrett?'

He pantomimed offence. 'That makes me sound like a Labrador.'

She pretended to consider the idea. 'No. Your ears aren't floppy enough.'

He couldn't help laughing. When was the last time he'd had this kind of fun, stretching a silly joke with someone?

'So have you been a good boy?' she asked again.

Teasing, huh? Two could play at that game. He lowered his voice to a purr. 'Oh, yes. I've been *very* good.' She went deliciously pink, and he laughed. 'Hey. You started it, Ms Lambert.'

'Hmm, well.' She batted her eyelashes at him. 'There's a bench over there, next to the fountain. Let's go and sit down.'

He was happy enough to hold her hand and stroll across the square to the bench. She delved into her handbag and brought out a small red cardboard box tied with a matching ribbon. 'I brought these for you. Only a couple, as they're quite rich,' she said.

He opened the box to discover two perfect

heart-shaped chocolates. The outer shell was perfectly glossy. 'They look fabulous. So the chocolate shell should be crisp to the bite, and the centre should be soft and rich?' he checked.

She nodded.

He took a bite, examined the centre, then finished the chocolate. He knew she was waiting to hear his response, so he left it until he could see she was practically wriggling with impatience. And then he said, 'Best chocolate ever. I'm going to save the other one until tomorrow—so I can savour it with a cup of coffee in my morning break.'

'Do you want me to put the box back in my handbag?' she asked.

'Thanks—that'd be great,' he said. 'Then it won't get squished in my pocket.' He looked at her. 'Did you enjoy the course?'

'Very much. Tomorrow, we're making ganache fillings and caramels, and working with finishes for hand-dipped chocolates—structure sheets for embossing the tops, transfers—they're made with coloured cocoa butter on acetate—gold lustre, piping with coloured cocoa butter, and textured inclusions.' She smiled. 'The course is definitely helping me to up my chocolate game.'

'That's great,' he said. 'Let's go and find a

bar, and I'd love to hear all about your favourite bits of the day and what you're planning to try on your customers when we're back in London.'

'And what about you? What have you been doing today?' she asked.

'Catching up with work, mainly. Sketching out a few ideas for a new client.'

'Obviously that's all confidential,' she said, 'but would I be right in thinking that's your favourite bit of your job?'

'One of them,' he said. 'It's looking at something and seeing all the possibilities, without any limits. Even crazy ideas you know would be completely impractical are useful, at this stage, because they might spark off something else.'

'Blue-sky thinking,' she said. 'Looking at something, deconstructing it, working out how it can become something else. It sounds a lot like what I do when I'm playing with a new dessert.'

He nodded. 'What if you change one element for another? What does the end customer really want and what's the best way of showing them what your client can offer?' He looked at her. 'I always believed I did my best thinking either walking in a park, or in the office, with everyone around me and their energy gelling with mine. But with video-conferencing you can have that feeling anywhere. And I discovered I like working in a sunny corner of a garden. Well, the roof terrace.'

'You don't have a garden, do you?' she asked.

'Usually I go for a walk in Hyde Park. But maybe,' he said, 'having my own green space, even if it's a roof terrace, is something I need to look at for the future.' And how crazy was it that all of a sudden he could see himself in a garden, with a dog stretched out on the patio in the sunshine, while he was pushing a small child on a swing? A small child with dark messy hair and huge brown eyes…

He shook himself.

He'd never thought about having a family of his own before. Why here? Why now?

Well, he knew some of the answers to that. Being here with Livi, seeing the genuine joy her family brought her—it made him want that sort of thing, too. That closeness. The connection that stretched from the past to the future.

Not that he intended to tell her that. Not yet, anyway. He needed to be careful not to scare her off, especially as he was halfway to scaring himself off.

They made their way through the streets of the old town and found a square with a large rectangular pond in the centre, with giant waterlilies floating in the centre.

'This must be some kind of art installation,' Livi said. She checked in her online guidebook. 'It is. Apparently they're made from mineral fibres which contain solar lighting.'

'They'll look pretty after dark, then,' Josh said.

She took a photograph. 'Even as they are now, they're pretty. And I could make a dessert based on that. Raspberry and lime,' she said. 'Maybe piped Italian meringue for the petals, and I'd be tempted to spray them.'

'It's fascinating, seeing the way your mind works,' Josh said. 'I look at those waterlilies and I think flowers: maybe Monet, maybe nice lighting. But you not only visualise the dessert, you know the flavours you want to use, too. That's amazing.'

'I guess it's just part of being a pastry chef,' she said. 'You get inspiration from all over the place. I might try a cocktail, and I'll deconstruct it into colours and flavours, and from there I'd think about what textures would work with those flavours to make a good dessert.'

'It's still an amazing skill,' he said.

They walked through the square, hand in hand, and then he spotted a bar with flower garlands outside; they took a peek inside, and discovered an enormous chalkboard with the cocktail menu, shelves containing beer bottles next to the specially shaped glasses matching the beer, and a selection of draught beer from a microbrewery which was apparently just round the corner.

'This looks fabulous,' she said.

'It does,' he agreed. 'What would you like?'

It took her a while to choose, but eventually she picked an espresso martini. 'It's an old favourite,' she said.

'I'll join you.'

They found a quiet table with comfortable bar stools, and she was thrilled when the waiter brought over what looked like two vintage martini glasses. 'And it's garnished properly, with three beans,' she said in satisfaction. 'The perfect presentation.'

He was enjoying talking through the menu with her, challenging her to make desserts out of the cocktails on the list, when he suddenly glimpsed something he hadn't noticed when they first came into the bar.

There was a stage at the back of the room.

A stage which now held a drum kit, amplifiers, a keyboard and a microphone.

He took a large gulp of his cocktail, but it wasn't enough to stop the darkness uncurling inside him. Particularly as there were four people walking onto the stage, two of them holding guitars.

'Josh?' One moment, he'd been laughing and joking with her, teasing her about how many different desserts she could possibly create out of any one given cocktail. And now his face was ashen. He seemed to be looking at something behind her. Frowning, she glanced round, and then she saw the band.

Oh, no.

She should've thought. It was Friday night. A lot of bars offered live music for their customers at the weekend. It was something she loved, but she also knew this had to be a nightmare for Josh.

She reached out to take his hand and squeeze it. 'Let's go.'

'I'm fine,' he said, though she could tell he was speaking through gritted teeth and he was very far from fine. 'We can stay. You've barely touched your drink.'

'That's not important,' she said gently. 'But you are. And this is too much for you, isn't it?'

He closed his eyes briefly and nodded.

'Then we'll go back to your hotel. Back to your lovely roof garden. Come on.'

They left their unfinished drinks and walked out of the bar just as the band started tuning up. The square was filled with people sitting at bistro tables on the little patios outside the various bars and restaurants, eating and drinking and chatting. She didn't bother trying to make a conversation with Josh because she felt that he needed the endorphins from walking more than anything else. He'd talk when he was ready. But she kept holding his hand, just so he'd know she wasn't deserting him.

Once they'd turned off the square into a quiet road, he said, 'I'm sorry. I've ruined the evening.'

'No, you haven't,' she reassured him. 'I get that it's hard for you.'

'I can tune out recorded stuff, most of the time,' he said. 'But not live music. Not when there are musicians working only a few metres away from me.'

'Doing what you used to do. Doing what you loved most in the world,' she said gently.

'It's like a hollow inside you, missing music, isn't it?'

'Yeah.' He looked at her. 'You're about the first person apart from my therapist who's ever really got that.'

But did that empty space also mean he was always going to protect his heart, keep people at a distance? He'd talked about getting to know her better, getting closer to her, but she remembered the last time they'd been really close. That night. He'd rejected her then; what was to stop him rejecting her again? Maybe she was the one who needed to be more careful of her heart.

Yet, at the same time, she couldn't just abandon him while he was hurting.

Maybe she needed to try telling him straight.

Back at his hotel, they took the lift up to his penthouse suite. There was a coffee machine with a selection of pods and a kettle with a range of teabags; she was pleased to note that they included her favourite blends.

'Go and sit on the terrace,' she said. 'I'm going to make us a mug of chamomile tea.' Once she'd brewed the tea, she carried the mugs out to the roof garden. Josh was sitting at the table, his face drawn with misery. Clearly the scent of the flowers and the prettiness of the fairy lights had done nothing to make him feel better.

He looked up as she approached. 'Thank you,' he said.

'No problem.' She set the mugs on the table and sat down opposite him. 'Josh, I'm going to give you some tough love. I think you need to get music back into your life. It's part of who you are and, even when you're putting on a smiling face to the world, you're so unhappy without it.' She reached over to take both his hands in hers. 'OK, the classical stuff might always be too hard. But there has to be a way. Music brought you so much joy. Could you do something without having to play? I guess that would rule out teaching, but could you produce, maybe? Compose?' She shook her head. 'I dunno—conduct, even?'

'I don't know,' he said. 'Where music's concerned…'

He'd built a wall between himself and what he'd loved most in the world, in an attempt to stop his heart breaking, Livi thought. And instead it had meant that his heart had been shut away. Was it to the point where he was unreachable?

'I get that,' she said, seeing the unhappiness etched into his face. 'But look at the life you've built outside music. You're good at your job. You're good at seeing what's missing, what needs to happen to make something work more effectively. Maybe you need to knock that brick wall down and combine your life now with music. Maybe you could help arts centres that are struggling?'

He made a noncommittal noise, and she knew he wasn't even going to consider it. As far as he was concerned, he'd bricked off the heart of his life, surrounded it in barbed wire, and he was always going to pretend things were fine when they weren't.

Even as she thought it, he straightened up a little. 'I'm sorry. This wasn't how this evening was meant to go. You were all bubbly about your course, and I loved listening to you. I wanted tonight to be all about cocktails and enjoying the crowds on a summer Friday evening.' He grimaced. 'If I'd spotted the stage, we could've had a drink somewhere else. Somewhere without live music. But I just saw a pretty little bar and I wanted to share it with you.'

'Maybe another night,' she said.

But he could see the disappointment in her face. And she'd had a point about getting music back into his life. It *was* part of who he was. He was utterly miserable without it. There was a yawning abyss inside him, as if he were hollowed out, and keeping that hidden from everyone else was wearing him out.

'You like dancing,' he said.

'Ye-es.' She looked wary.

Even though the idea made him feel almost sick with nerves, Livi was the one person who might understand. And here, on this quiet roof terrace, filled with roses and fairy lights, he could maybe be the person she needed him to be, too. 'Dance with me now?' he asked.

'Hang on. You're asking me to dance with you?' She blinked.

He had enough doubts of his own, but he was going to try. 'I'm assuming you have an app. A playlist of some sort. Something soft and slow. Something you love listening to.'

'Well, yes.' She'd obviously worked out that he was trying to follow her suggestion, because her face brightened with hope. 'There's a singer my mum and I really love—Mum used to play him all the time when Eti and I were small, and ever since I've been old enough to go to gigs I always get tickets to see him with Mum for his UK tour. He always does a couple of acoustic numbers in a gig—minimal guitar or piano. Could we dance to that?'

He appreciated that she was trying her best to minimise the instruments. For her, he was going to try his hardest to make this work. Not trusting himself to speak, he nodded.

She quickly found the playlist on her phone, slipped one earbud into her ear and handed him the other. He stared at the earbud as if it were a poisonous asp she'd asked him to put into his ear, but then he gritted his teeth and did it.

'Are you sure about this?' she checked.

No. 'Yes,' he fibbed. 'I'm a bit out of practice.' If he was honest with himself, he could barely ever remember dancing with a girlfriend. He'd never been one for clubbing, even before the accident. People didn't really dance to the kind of music he played. They listened to it. *Felt* it.

He forced himself not to think about that. This was different. This was for Livi.

'No need for fancy steps,' she said. 'Just hold me and sway.' She started the track and slipped the phone into her pocket, then stepped close to him, sliding her arms round his neck.

He remained frozen for a few more moments—but then he wrapped his arms round her waist, drawing her closer, and finally, finally, he swayed to the rhythm of the song with her.

He held her as if he were drowning and she were his lifeline.

Slowly, her warmth relaxed him enough to unstiffen his shoulders and release his grip so he was cradling her.

He could feel the rhythm of the dance, the slow, gentle softness of it, and it felt as if something was cracking inside him. Breaking through all the barriers he'd put up over the last eight years, letting his heart out of the confines where he'd tried to keep it safe but had only succeeded in imprisoning himself.

She sang softly along with the track, and it felt as if she was singing to him. Words of love and comfort and desire and promise. And after all the years of keeping himself rigidly away from music, everything was fluid and strange, spinning a whirlpool of emotions round him.

He desperately wanted to kiss her, but they were supposed to be taking things slowly and he didn't want to push her away. His voice felt rusty; he couldn't even remember the last time he'd sung anything, but he'd picked up the structure of the tune—it always had been like that for him with music, and he had an almost photographic memory for it—and he remembered the words of the chorus. When the second verse ended, he sang the chorus to her.

This time it was Livi's turn to freeze for a moment. Josh was pretty sure she was panicking that she'd pushed him too far, so he held her close and kept swaying with her in time to the music.

A tear trickled down her cheek and he kissed it away. 'It's OK, Livi. It's all going to be OK.'

And then somehow his mouth had moved from her cheek to the corner of her mouth, and then to a proper kiss; she was kissing him back, and everything felt very all right with the world.

He kissed her through another track, feeling as if his heart was breaking out of the darkness at last.

But then the next track started, and after the first few seconds of acoustic guitar a string quartet started playing.

It felt as if the glass wall round his heart had suddenly shattered and the shards embedded deeply. Too deeply for him to be able to do this.

He broke the kiss. Stopped holding her. Stood there, frozen.

'I can't do this, Livi,' he whispered. 'I *can't.*'

Her face was filled with anguish, and she switched off the music. 'I'm so sorry, Josh. I forgot this one had the v—' She broke off the word, biting her lip. 'Josh.'

'I can't do this.' He shook his head, trying to clear it, but he couldn't. And he knew what the problem was. Him. He couldn't offer her what she needed, his whole heart. The black hole was still inside him and it was never going away. And it wouldn't be fair to pull her into this misery with him.

Maybe he should tell her what nearly happened, the night she knocked on the door of his flat. But then she'd pity him. And, worse, she might feel obliged to stay with him in case that particular darkness threatened to overwhelm him again. He didn't want her to be with him out of pity.

So he kept the words inside. Even though they were trying to burst out.

'I'm sorry, Livi,' he said. 'This isn't working. And it's not you—it's me.'

It's not you—it's me.

The ultimate break-up phrase, Livi thought.

It was supposed to soften the blow and make the dumpee feel better—but it didn't. All it really meant was that the person doing the dumping didn't want to explain their real reasons.

So much for thinking all her dreams were finally coming true—that Josh was prepared to make the effort and they actually had a real shot at a future, at being together.

Though maybe he had a point. Maybe she should stop harking back to that old teenage dream. Because what sort of life would they have if she had to spend all her time treading on eggshells, worrying that something would remind him of what he'd lost and drive him back into despair—and knowing that she wasn't enough to fill the empty spaces inside him?

'I'd better go,' she said dully.

'I'll walk you back,' he said.

She shook her head. 'No need. It's not far, and it's on the main streets.'

'I'm sorry,' he said. 'I…' He blew out a breath. 'I'm still a mess. It's not your fault, and it's not your responsibility to fix me. I'm the one who needs to sort it out.'

That was all true; but she wished he hadn't drawn her close again, only to back away.

Last time, she felt that he'd blamed her.

This time, he was at least accepting the

fault was his; but he'd still hurt her. Led her to believe in a dream that had burst at the first stroke of a bow across a violin string.

'Good night, Josh,' she said. Though it felt much more final than that. It felt like *goodbye*.

She picked up her handbag. Then she quietly walked away from him through the French doors to his hotel suite, through the front door, and she let it click quietly closed behind her before trudging across Grand-Place to her hotel. She didn't notice the beautifully lit buildings, the crowds of people chatting and drinking and dancing. All she could see was Josh standing there, drowning in misery—and there was nothing, *nothing* she could do to fix it.

He'd said it wasn't her responsibility to fix him. But oh, how she'd wanted to fix him.

He'd wanted to dance with her—for her sake, knowing she loved it. He'd tried to share her kind of music. And, for those first few moments of dancing together, she'd really thought he'd felt the joy and not the pain. He'd let the music flow over him and he'd reacted. He'd held her, danced with her, sung to her, kissed her…

And then the whole thing had imploded.

If only it had been another song playing next, one without the romantic addition of a string quartet. But she had to be honest: if it hadn't happened tonight, it would've happened some time soon. And it would've hurt more, having what she truly believed was their future snatched away again.

They didn't have a future. She had to face it: Josh wasn't ready to start a proper relationship. Not with her—not with anyone. He'd locked his heart back up again. Pushed her away. Told her it wasn't going to work between them. This time, he hadn't been cruel; but this time, his rejection felt final. There was no coming back.

Back at the hotel, she went through the motions of showering and making herself a mug of chamomile tea. She barely tasted it, and it did nothing to help her sleep. She lay awake, too miserable to cry, going over and over in her head what she could've said or done to make a difference.

And the truth was, there was nothing she could've said. Nothing she could've done. Josh was implacable.

She had no idea how the brasserie project was going to work, now. Would he back out of it completely, or would he do what he'd suggested to her weeks ago and hand it over to one of his team? She'd been so looking forward to this: working with him, starting a new chapter in the history of Lambert's—a new chapter in her life, perhaps.

But now she knew it wasn't going to happen.

It was over.

CHAPTER THIRTEEN

WHEN THE FRONT door clicked quietly behind her, it felt like the worst day of Josh's life, all over again. Last time, he'd lost what he lived for doing. This time, he'd lost the woman he fallen in love with: but he knew it was all his own fault. He'd pushed her away. She'd given him a second chance, but he'd blown it.

Because he'd rushed things.

Because he wasn't truly ready to move on.

Because locking the pain away inside him wasn't the same as dealing with it. Instead, he'd made himself more vulnerable when he'd finally had to face music, and Livi had been the collateral damage. He'd been unfair to her—and he needed to do something about it. It was too late to ring London now, but luckily he'd bought an open return and could take the first train back tomorrow. And on the train he'd start to make the arrangements he needed.

In the morning, he packed, not bothering with breakfast beyond a mug of coffee, checked out of the hotel, and headed for London. He made the phone call that he hoped would start to change everything; then, once the week in rehab was arranged, he let Shelley know that he needed to be away for a week and arranged for one of his colleagues to handle the Lambert account in his absence.

Next, he messaged Sophie and Michel, to let them know that he was stepping back from the project for personal reasons but his colleague would look after them.

Back at the mews house, he packed, then rang his parents to let them know what he was doing.

Even though part of him desperately wanted to contact Livi, he didn't. Until he'd got through the next week and could be sure that things were changing—that he really could handle this—it wouldn't be fair to keep her hanging on.

And then he put his case in the car. This wasn't going to be a quick fix. But he hoped he'd make enough progress this week to prove to himself—and Livi—that he was going to give it his best shot.

Somehow, Livi managed to concentrate on the final day of her course. Josh didn't contact her.

He didn't answer his phone when she called him at the end of the course, but she didn't leave a message—because what, just *what*, could she say? This was something that would definitely be better in person. She walked to his hotel, only to find that he'd checked out.

Well, that was pretty final. Not only had he rejected her, he'd left the city without saying anything to her. He really couldn't make it any clearer that he didn't want her.

Brussels had lost its sparkle for her without Josh. She couldn't even finish the comfort food of a sausage and *stoemp* in the nice little bar round the corner from her hotel. It seemed pointless staying in the city tomorrow just for the sake of it, so she changed her train ticket for an earlier departure, and left for London on Sunday morning.

She'd just unpacked and set a load of laundry going when her door intercom buzzed. For a moment, she wondered if it was Josh—if the almost two days they'd spent apart had given him enough space to change his mind. But when she answered, she recognised her mother's voice instantly.

'Hey, Mum. Come up,' she said, and pressed the intercom to release the door.

'How was Brussels?' Sophie asked.

'I really enjoyed the course,' Livi said, 'and I went to the bar where great-granddad Jean worked. I sent Dad the photographs. And I bought a square of lace very like the kind of thing great-great-grandma Marie-Thérèse would've made.' She took the large gold ballotin box from her kitchen worktop and gave it to her mother. 'These are for you and Dad. Made by me, from scratch, with love. Pralines, ganaches and caramels.'

'Thank you, darling.' Sophie hugged her. 'Do you want to talk about it?'

'The course?' Livi asked, deliberately misunderstanding her. 'Sure. Though maybe I should wait until Dad's free, as well.'

Sophie coughed. 'You know perfectly well I don't mean the course.'

Livi sighed. 'Mum, there's nothing to tell. Josh has made up his mind. It's over.'

'He messaged us yesterday,' Sophie said. 'He's stepping back from the brasserie project and one of his team is taking over.'

Livi closed her eyes for a moment. 'I had a feeling he might do that. OK. I guess it's easier that way.' For both of them.

'So what happened?'

Livi swallowed hard. 'He's still broken, Mum. Without his music, he's not fully himself, and I don't think he can really give his heart to anyone until he's whole.' She told her mum what had happened, her voice catching as she struggled to hold back her emotion. 'I thought he'd be able to cope with an acoustic set. Just a voice and a guitar. The recording from the show we went to at the Royal Albert Hall, last year. But I forgot one of the songs had a string quartet playing. And he…' She dragged in a breath. 'Then he said he couldn't do this. That it was his fault, not mine.'

Sophie winced. 'Oh, darling.'

'I left. I wouldn't even let him walk me back to the hotel. It's over.' She blinked back the tears. 'I really thought we had something, Mum. I liked who he'd become. He liked me. I thought we…' She shook her head. 'Well, I was wrong.'

'I'm sorry,' Sophie said. 'I shouldn't have interfered and told him where you were.'

'If it hadn't happened then,' Livi said, 'it would've happened another time. It's not your fault. It's not anyone's, really,' she added, 'because Josh can't help how he feels.'

'That,' Sophie said, 'is incredibly generous of you.'

'There's no point in being bitter about it,' Livi said. 'I'm going to pick myself up, dust myself down, and—well, just carry on. Moping isn't going to make me feel better. I'd rather keep myself busy.'

'Just remember I'm always here,' Sophie said, and hugged her. 'Come down for dinner. Or I can bring something up to you.'

Livi smiled. 'I'm fine, Mum. I promise.'

After Sophie had gone back to the restaurant, Livi finished unpacking. But, while she was putting things away, she came across the letter Josh had written her all those years ago. The letter she'd never opened.

Maybe it was time she read it.

She slit the envelope, then sat on the end of her bed and read what he had to say.

Things he'd actually said to her, face to face, over the last couple of weeks. That he was truly sorry for the unkind things he'd said. They weren't true and he'd lashed out at her from a place of darkness. But he was truly grateful to her, because without her he wouldn't be here now.

She frowned. What did he mean by that?

Not that there was any point in asking him. She was pretty sure he wouldn't answer.

She turned back to the letter. Thanks to her, he said, he was going to get some proper help.

And he hoped she'd be happy in the future, surrounded by people who loved her.

The words were sincere, and the heartbreak was visible in every stroke of the pen. He'd got some help, yes, but it hadn't been enough. Because he was still too damaged to offer her what she needed—his heart.

A week later, Josh walked into Covent Garden, wondering if he was doing the right thing. Should he just let Livi go, and hope she'd find the happiness he hadn't been able to give her?

Then again, faint heart never won fair lady. And the whole point of the last week had been to stop being a coward. To face things. To get himself on a path where he'd deserve all the love Livi had to give, and give her all the love she deserved in return.

Maybe he should've told her what he was doing. Texted her, called her. Except this was something he wanted to tell her face to face. He wanted her to be able to look him in the eye and see that he was sincere.

If she'd let him.

He took a deep breath, walked up to the door at Lambert's Brasserie, and pushed it open. It was still relatively early, but there were several tables of people eating breakfast. Clearly the new brunch menu was a hit. Good. At least he'd helped her to achieve one of her dreams. Even if he had managed to break her heart in the meantime.

Sophie was on front of house. She narrowed her eyes at him. This was starting to be a pattern, he thought. One he needed to break.

'Joshua,' she said, her voice very cool. 'What can we do for you?'

'A very, very big ask,' he said. 'I'd like to talk to Livi.'

'If you're going to let her down yet again,' Sophie said, 'then I'd prefer you not to.'

'I'm not going to let her down,' Josh said. 'I owe her another apology—but I also owe her an explanation. All I want to do is talk.'

'Wait here, and I'll ask her,' Sophie said with a sigh. 'Though I expect you to abide by her decision.'

'That's fair,' Josh said.

He waited.

And waited some more.

And just when he thought that Sophie was about to come back and tell him that Livi didn't want anything to do with him, Livi herself walked out into the restaurant.

She looked tired and a little bit sad, and his heart ached.

'You wanted to see me,' she said, and her voice was completely expressionless. Which he knew he deserved, because hadn't he rejected her twice, now?

'Yes. Would you walk with me?' he asked.

'Fifteen minutes,' she warned.

'Thank you,' he said.

Stallholders were still setting up in the market, but he had somewhere quiet in mind, only a couple of minutes from the restaurant: the small gardens behind St Paul's church, which weren't really on tourists' radar and at this time of year they were the kind of place he thought Livi would like, filled with roses and hollyhocks.

Just as he'd hoped, most of the wooden benches lining the path were empty.

He chose the one furthest from anyone else. 'Shall we sit?'

'What's this about, Josh?' she asked, but to his relief she sat on the bench and he joined her.

'An apology,' he said. 'An explanation. And…' He shook his head. 'No, I'm getting ahead of myself. First off, I want to apologise. Sincerely. You're right. I was still broken, and I was lying to myself as well as everyone else. I thought I could just wall off that bit of me and carry on. But I can't—and it's up to me to fix that, nobody else.'

She looked wary, but at least she was listening.

'I've spent the last week away in rehab,' he said. 'I've done a lot of talking—to a therapist—and a lot of thinking. I'm not there, yet, but I'm in a much better place than I was.'

'That's why you left Brussels? To go to therapy?'

The hurt was obvious in her voice. 'I should've told you I was going,' he said. 'I'm sorry for that, too. But I felt I'd already done you enough damage. I didn't want to give you false hope. I went to start fixing myself. Which is *my* responsibility, nobody else's,' he added. 'It's going to take a while, but I'm working on it and I can see I've made progress. I intend to keep going.'

She gave a single brief nod.

'And I owe you an explanation. One that stems right back to *that* night,' he said. 'Apart from telling my therapist last week, I haven't talked to anyone else about it. Ever. My parents and your brother don't know, so I'd appreciate it if you kept this confidential—I don't want them to be hurt.'

She was silent for a moment, but finally said, 'All right.'

'And I apologise in advance,' he said, 'because I know this is going to be difficult to hear. It's difficult to say out loud, or write, or even admit in my head. But I need to be honest and open with you, Livi. I need to stop hiding.'

'I'm listening,' she said.

'I'd hit rock bottom, back then. Everything I'd always wanted was gone. I didn't have any hope left. I was miserable, and I just wanted the pain to stop,' he said. 'I had a bottle of sleeping tablets. I was psyching myself up to take them.'

Her face lost all its colour. 'You were going to…?'

Clearly she couldn't face saying the words. He understood that feeling. It had been so hard to say it out loud; but telling her had been easier. 'Yes, I was,' he said, and his voice shook slightly as he remembered the despair he'd felt. How close he'd been. 'But then you knocked on my door. And I kissed you. And that kiss made me remember that there was stuff in the world that was good—that life wasn't just unending pain.'

'Oh, my God. I didn't have a…' She shook her head. 'I don't know what to say. Except I'm glad you didn't take the sleeping tablets. And that also explains what you said in your letter.'

He blinked. 'You read it?'

'Last week. It was about time.' She paused. 'You said without me, you wouldn't be here now, and I didn't understand what you meant.' Her eyes glistened with unshed tears. 'Now, I think I do.'

'I didn't tell you about it to make you have sympathy for me or pity me,' he said. 'I told you because I owe it to you to be honest. Last time I did therapy, I still kept too much back. I thought I could manage it on my own, and all I did was block it off instead of dealing with it. And my arrogance meant that you got hurt. For that, I'm truly sorry.'

Again, she didn't speak, just nodded.

'I want to change,' he said. 'You're right. Without music in my life, there's always going to be an empty space inside me. And it's not fair to make everyone else in my life feel they have to be super-cautious all the time in case they do or say something that reminds me.' He swallowed hard. 'I'm not sure if I'm ever going to get to the point where I can see someone else perform the three solos that were my signature, but I can do the rest of it. I'm getting the help I need. I want to dance with you,

Livi, in a moonlit garden or on the beach. I want to feel the joy of music again, with you right by my side. But most of all I want you by my side. I know I've treated you badly, and I wouldn't blame you for refusing to give me another chance. But I'm trying to open my heart to you, and I'm really hoping that you have room in your heart to forgive me.' And now was when he really needed to tell her everything. 'But music isn't the love of my life anymore.'

'It's not?'

'It's not,' he said gently. 'It's you.'

She blinked. 'You love me?'

'I think I've loved you for a long time,' he said. 'I always saw you as Eti's little sister, and I knew you were too young for anything to happen between us—but I kind of always knew you were there.'

'With my stupid schoolgirl crush.'

The words he'd used as a weapon, all those years ago. He really *had* hurt her. He winced. 'That was unfair of me.'

'You were right, actually. It *was* a schoolgirl crush,' she said. 'I didn't really know you. And I got over it. But then you walked back into my life, and I discovered I liked the man you'd become. You weren't this slightly-out-of-reach superstar anymore. I thought we had a real chance for a future—but then you rejected me again.'

'I think,' he said, 'I was rejecting *me* rather than rejecting you. I didn't feel I could offer you what you needed. And that in itself was arrogant and stupid, because I should've asked you what you wanted, and whether you'd maybe be prepared to settle for me as a compromise.'

'Settle? For you?' She rolled her eyes. 'Do you not see the way women look at you, Josh?'

'No,' he said honestly. 'And I don't actually care how women look at me. I do care about how you look at me, though. And I'm sorry I let the stuff in my head get in the way of us.' This time, he had the courage to reach out and take her hand. 'I'm not perfect, Livi. I'm a work in progress—but I really do mean to work on my issues and get better. Because I want everything, and I want to give you everything. I want all of you.'

'That's a mite greedy,' she said.

But then he noticed that the corners of her eyes had crinkled, and realised she was teasing him. Pricking his pomposity.

'Yeah, it is,' he agreed. 'But I want to be with you, Livi. I want a family. I never even knew that until we were in Brussels, and we talked about me not having a garden—but I had this clear vision of pushing a little girl on a swing, and a dog on the patio. A little girl who looked like you.'

'You want children?'

He couldn't quite read what she wanted. He could see doubts, but he wasn't sure why. 'If we're lucky, and only if you want that, too,' he said. Just so she'd know he wasn't taking her for granted. 'I see four generations of talent with food stretching over the years in your family. I'd like to see that continue to the next generation, and the next.'

'What if,' she asked, 'we have children and they inherit *your* talent instead of mine? What if they're a classical musical prodigy? Are you going to shut down their talent, or refuse to go to a single performance?'

It was a fair question, and now he understood her doubts. He'd known other musicians who hadn't had family support. Nobody there to catch their eye and give them a smile to push the stage nerves away. It wouldn't be quite like that for his own child—for a start, Livi would be there, plus her entire family and his parents.

But he wanted to be there, too. To give his child the same unwavering love and support he'd had. And to teach them to have a better balance in their life so they never put their talent above true love.

'No,' he said. 'I'd want to be there.' He took a deep breath. 'But more importantly I want to be right by your side.'

'So how do we do this?' she asked.

'Together,' he said. 'We take the rough with the smooth. I'm afraid there's probably going to be a bit more rough than smooth until I've done some more work with the therapist,' he admitted, 'but I truly believe I can do it, with you by my side.' He paused. 'But that's only if you want to be there.'

'Are you asking me?'

'I'm asking you,' he said. 'Will you give me a second chance to put you first?'

'I don't actually want you to put me first,' she said. 'Just as I don't want to put you first, either. I want us to be *together*. As equals.'

'That,' he said, 'sounds perfect.'

And at long, long last, he kissed her.

EPILOGUE

Two years later

JOSH SAT IN the back of the black cab with Livi, on their way from the mews house in Bayswater to St Martin-in-the-Fields. The classical concert tonight contained some of his favourite pieces, Bach's *Concerto for two violins* and the *Air on a G string*. Pieces he'd once enjoyed playing and had shut out of his life for years, but now he could enjoy listening to them again.

Livi had been right. Having his music back had given him his heart back, too. To the point where he could give his whole heart to her.

They'd both blossomed, over the last two years. Lambert's Brasserie had expanded to two more restaurants and a thriving café; and Livi had won awards for her chocolates, exquisite flavour paired with exquisite artistry. JGA had taken on new clients in the music business, including a music therapy charity;

working with them had helped Josh solidify his progress in bringing music back to his life.

They'd got married a year ago—with Livi wearing a lace veil based on her great-grandmother's wedding veil and their wedding cake's design echoing the lace—and the photograph was still the one on the Lambert's social media with the most hits.

Josh couldn't imagine being any happier than he was right now. He particularly cherished their once-a-month family Sunday lunches where both sets of parents came over, as well as Etienne, Lucy and little Louisa; he cooked the mains and Livi produced the show-stopping desserts. And everyone talked until they were hoarse, played games and just enjoyed spending time together. Two years ago, he wouldn't have even dreamed of this perfect life. This perfect team.

She squeezed his hand. 'OK?' she checked.

'Yes.' He wasn't going to admit to the slight twitchiness he felt before the concert, because he knew he could cope with anything with Livi by his side. 'You?'

'I've been thinking about expanding,' she said.

'A second café? Or do you have your eyes on that vacant shop round the corner?'

'Chocolate shop? We could,' she said. 'But

I have something slightly different in mind.' She gave him the sweetest, sweetest smile, and took a box from her handbag.

It was the size and shape of a small chocolate bar, and it was secured with a ribbon tied in a bow. She sometimes left chocolate experiments on his desk, wrapped like this. But what did it have to do with expanding?

'What's this?' he asked.

'Open it,' she said.

He untied the ribbon, then opened the box.

And then he simply stared.

It was a bar of glossy milk chocolate. But not just any old bar: this one had a sketch drawn in white chocolate. A sketch of what looked like a pregnancy test. In the little flat section that would show the test result, there was writing in ruby chocolate piping. The words were very distinct and clear.

Pregnant 3

Was she telling him…?

He stared at her. 'Livi?'

She nodded. 'I did it this morning. The kit's at home, and I took a picture. But I thought this might be a nicer way to tell you. A one-off design,' she added casually.

'You're pregnant. We're having a baby.' He was almost too stunned to take it in. Gently, wanting to protect the chocolate from snapping in half accidentally, he slid it back into the box, then slid the box into his pocket. And then he wrapped his arms round her and kissed her. 'We're having a baby,' he said in wonder. 'You and me. That's amazing.'

'Boy or girl, single or twins, cook or musician or marketing CEO—or something we haven't even thought about yet,' she said.

'Whoever they are, they'll be loved more than any baby's been loved before,' Josh said, meaning every word. 'This is the icing on the cake.'

'Icing on the chocolate bar,' she corrected with a grin.

He laughed. Livi's puns were terrible, but since she'd been back in his life the laughter had been back, too. And most definitely the love. 'I love you,' he said softly. 'You and our baby-to-be. You're the world to me.'

She kissed him back. 'You're the world to me, too.'

And Josh knew that everything was going to be just fine.

* * * * *

If you enjoyed this story, check out these other great reads from Kate Hardy

The Surgeon's Tropical Temptation
His Strictly Off-Limits Ballerina
Paediatrician's Unexpected Second Chance
A Fake Bride's Guide to Forever

All available now!